GOOD VIBES ONLY

SHORT STORIES FROM IRON ON IRON

GREGORY ASHE

H&B

Good Vibes Only
Copyright © 2024 Gregory Ashe

Published by Hodgkin & Blount
https://www.hodgkinandblount.com/
contact@hodgkinandblount.com

Published 2024
Printed in the United States of America

Version 1.03

Trade Paperback ISBN: 978-1-63621-073-5
eBook ISBN: 978-1-63621-072-8

All the Feels

This story takes place after *The Face in the Water*.

1

"You can stay as long as you want," John-Henry Somerset said as he took the steps to the porch and unlocked the front door.

His husband, Emery Hazard, said, "No, you can't."

Jem was trying to catch Tean's eye. Tean ignored him.

The town reminded Tean, in some ways, of Provo before Utah had grown up—the tree-lined streets; the older, well-kept homes; the college anchoring the community. But, of course, it wasn't Utah. So many bars, for one thing. So many coffee shops, for another. The house, though, could have come from Provo's Center Street: a two-story Arts and Crafts, old but lovingly kept up. The smell of microwaved pizza met them as they stepped inside, and somewhere nearby a dog began to bark.

"Hsst," Jem hissed.

"Colt," Emery called toward the back of the house.

Tean kicked Jem's foot while John-Henry was distracted with the luggage.

"Colt!" Turning back to them, Emery shrugged. "He might be asleep."

"Is he sick?" Tean asked. To Emery's uncomprehending look, he added, "It's two o'clock."

"You could say he's been dealing with this particular illness since he turned thirteen," John-Henry said with a wry smile. "He'll recover. Give him a few more years."

"He's not ill," Emery said. "He's a teenager." At that moment, a dog — a puppy, Tean realized — came sliding around the corner, nails scrabbling for purchase on the floorboards. She caught herself, corrected course, and came barreling toward them, yapping. "I see the goddamn dog managed not to get lost while we were gone."

"Your daughter loves that dog," John-Henry said. "Something you might want to remember."

Emery set his jaw and, to Tean's amazement, scooped the puppy up and began to give it pets.

"Sleeping until two sounds amazing," Jem said. "In the good old days, before I met Tean, I could sleep until ten, eleven o'clock in the morning. Later if I'd gone out the night before."

"When?" Tean asked.

"In the bad old days."

"Uh huh."

"Also, psst."

Tean tried to imagine a scenario where transporting his husband inside a suitcase would be acceptable. There had to be some sort of moral escape clause when necessity demanded.

"Do you have something caught in your throat?" Emery asked.

"Nope," Jem said with a grin.

"Come on. I'll show you to your room."

"I'm going to finish unloading the car," John-Henry said. "Send Colt out when you find him."

Still carrying the dog, Emery started toward the back of the house.

Jem opened his mouth.

"If you say hiss or p—"

"You were about to say piss, weren't you?"

"—or anything, I'm going to make you help John-Henry unload the car."

"Teancum Leon!"

"I'll do it."

"That sounds like a chore!"

"Try me."

"I was going to say whisper-whisper."

"Goodbye."

Jem, of course, trailed after Tean as he followed Emery.

The hallway ended in a spacious living room with an opening that connected to the kitchen. A blanket lay tangled on the sofa, covered in the kind of red marks that Tean associated with ultraprocessed snack foods, often of the mouth-scorchingly hot variety. At least six different pairs of sneakers lay kicked around the room in various places. There was an odor, not quite covered up by the smell of microwaved pizza, that reminded Tean of the youth camps he occasionally volunteered at over the summer.

Emery was already starting up a flight of stairs, bellowing, "Colt, God damn it, where are you?"

No answer.

"We can stay at a hotel," Jem said as he tagged along.

"We can't afford to stay at a hotel. Not for a week."

"We can find a way to afford it."

Tean stopped on the first step and looked back at his husband.

"Legally," Jem said. "Mostly legally. Fifty percent."

"We agreed—"

"No, please."

"—when we discussed the possibility of extending our stay—"

"Not the word. Not that word."

"—that our budget—"

Jem groaned and melted against the wall.

"—meant not staying in a hotel or a motel—"

"I'm dying I'm dead. I'm literally dead, slained by my own husband."

"It's just slain. And you need to knock it off; they'll have their feelings hurt. They're excited we're here."

"Get your ass out of bed, that's why!" Emery roared above them.

"We can get a suite," Jem whispered.

"No."

"It can have four rooms. Eight rooms. Fine, fine, it will have sixteen rooms, and one of them can have a giant TV, and you can watch your favorite movie about those two deer that are bad roommates. One of them's named Buck."

"It's not a movie. It's footage from a camera trap. And I only watched it that one time.'

Jem gave him a look.

"Twice, but only because the way that one shed his velvet was so interesting—stop it! I know what you're doing. We're staying here. As long as they'll let us. Because they're being generous, and we need—"

"Why can't you just leave me alone?" That voice was new—warbling on the edge of manhood, volume set to ear splitting. "I was trying to sleep!"

"Because it's two o'clock in the afternoon and the house is a sty! Get up and do your chores!"

A door slammed, the sound shotgunning through the house. A moment later, a boy in his late teens appeared at the top of the stairs. He was tall, still thin the way many teenagers are, but his body taking on the shape and mass of adulthood. His hair was bushy, verging on hedgehog territory, and his eyes were that same startling autumn gold as Emery's. When they lit on Jem and Tean, fresh disgust filled his features.

He came down the stairs two at a time, twisting his body to get past Tean.

"Hey," Jem said, sticking out a hand, "I'm—"

The boy stormed into the kitchen, and a moment later, another door slammed shut.

"Let me guess," John-Henry said from the entry hall. "You met Colt."

Emery started down the steps, clearly in pursuit of the boy. "Room's on the right. Enjoy your stay. Every day here is a fucking treat."

2

Jem wasn't allowed to play the Xbox; that's what Tean had said. And he wasn't allowed to go through any of Emery's or John-Henry's private things. He wasn't even allowed in their room, not even when nobody else was upstairs, not even if he promised he could put everything back so they'd never notice.

"Read your book," Tean said.

"I've already finished it."

"You've read it a dozen times. You love that book."

"It's *Night of the Living Dummy*, Tean, not *War and Peace*. I've had shits that take longer to finish."

That made Tean look up from his book. "You have?"

"That was a joke."

"Because if your bowel movements—"

"Stop."

It looked, from where Jem was lying on the narrow double bed in the cramped bedroom that was clearly supposed to be an office, like Tean had to wrestle to let that one go.

"What about your other book?"

"I don't want to read. I want to go out and do something."

The rap on the door made Jem prop himself up on one elbow.

"Come in," Tean called.

John-Henry had changed into sweat shorts and a sleeveless tee; the tats were on full display. "You don't have to stay up here, you know. I mean, if you want some privacy, that's fine, but we'd love to have you hang out with us."

"We're fine—" Tean began.

"Yes, God, thank you."

Jem didn't actually do a flying dismount, but his last bounce off the mattress might have been, to judge by Tean's look, a little overenthusiastic.

Downstairs, Colt stood at the kitchen counter, riffling a deck of playing cards. A dark-haired girl, who must have been around the same age as Anahí, was lining up stuffed animals on the couch. She had John-Henry's features with darker coloring, but the intense focus on her face reminded Jem of a certain grumpy detective. Through the window, Jem could see the puppy zooming back and forth in the yard, apparently living her best puppy life.

"Put whatever you want to watch on TV," John-Henry said. "Want something to drink? Make yourself at home—the pantry's here, fridge, cups and plates are up here."

Colt looked up from the cards long enough to give them a considering look. Then he noticed Jem looking back, set his jaw in a scowl, and turned his attention back to the cards. He was trying to do a card spring flourish, which was a cool trick if you could pull it off. Colt was apparently still learning, though, because the cards sprayed everywhere. A hint of color rose in his cheeks, and he resolutely did not look at them as he gathered them up.

Evie, on the other hand, did look at them. She was staring at them with a child's total disregard for social norms, obviously trying to figure them out. Tean smiled and gave her a wave, and she stone-faced him. Jem had to hide a grin at that. Then she grabbed a book and sprinted toward John-Henry.

"Daddy, will you read this to me?"

John-Henry scooped her up, a Diet Pepsi in one hand, and carried her over to the couch. He sat, dramatically forcing an opening between the stuffed animals, which made Evie scream and laugh in a mixture of outrage and delight.

"Go for it," John-Henry said, nodding at the TV.

"I'll read my book," Tean said. "Do you want me to put something on for you?"

"Jem?" John-Henry asked.

"You're holding the cards too tightly," Jem said, "and then, when you let go, you're too loose."

Colt glanced at him.

"He'll be fine," Tean said with something that sounded suspiciously like a sigh.

"Here," Jem said.

For a moment, Colt only watched him warily. Then he passed over the cards.

Jem cut the deck, shuffled them, played around with the cards — little stuff, the kind of showboating that gave you a feel for the deck and, at the same time, impressed the hell out of people who didn't know anything about cards. It worked even in Missouri, apparently, because Colt's eyes got huge.

"You're trying to do this, right?" Jem asked as he did the spring.

"Holy shit!" Colt said.

"Language," John-Henry said. Evie said something, and he answered, "No, honey. Peter's going to be fine. Farmer McGregor won't get him."

Tean cleared his throat.

Jem decided to ignore that particular trouble that was brewing. Instead, he focused on Colt as he handed back the cards. "Let's see your grip. Nope. Move your pinky — yeah, that's better."

"It feels like the cards are going to fall."

"Well, you want them to get out of your hand, right? Go ahead and —" The cards did a dismal spring, which was more like an erratic dribble, but Jem grinned. "That was better."

"Can you show me?"

Jem took the cards back and demonstrated the grip again. "Why are you learning how to do this? I thought kids your age only played Xbox."

"Well, honey, Peter shouldn't have disobeyed his mother," John-Henry was saying. "Ask Mr. Tean. He's a veterinarian."

"That's actually kind of true," Tean said. "Many rabbits are orphaned, which drastically reduces their rate of survival. As few as ten percent of orphaned rabbits survive —"

Out of a general sense of morality and goodishness, Jem took pity on John-Henry. More specifically, for the look on John-Henry's face. "Bandersnatch! Bandersnatch!"

John-Henry stared at him.

Tean stared at him.

Colt stared at him.

"That's, like, our safe word," Jem told him. "Only for conversations."

"It is not," Tean said. "We don't have a — that isn't a — we never —"

Colt pulled his tee up over his mouth as he laughed.

"Let me show you a hot shot cut," Jem said. "You're not there yet, but it looks dope, and it'll give you something to work toward after you get the spring down." He did the cut, catching the lone card he spun out of the deck. Colt's eyes got huge again, and he forgot about the shirt, letting it drop. Again.

"He's only a little bit sick," John-Henry was saying. "It's a cold, and he'll drink his chamomile tea and feel better."

"The real concern," Tean began, "would be GI stasis. Or, of course, cancer."

Jem registered the problem, but he was having too much fun to give it his full attention. "If you practice with a buddy —" Jem repeated the cut, only this time, he directed the card at Colt, who fumbled and then caught it. "—you can have him catch the card, which is the perfect opportunity for you to do something like this." He held up Colt's wallet, which he'd snagged while the boy had been occupied with the cards.

"That's leaving out dental disease," Tean said.

"Tean," John-Henry said, his voice tense, "I'm reading a children's book."

"Oh. Right. Well, GI stasis is when a rabbit's tummy stops working, often with fatal —"

"Tean!" John-Henry took a breath. "Jeez."

Jem glanced over; Tean's face was red, his eyes full of surprise that transmuted into hurt.

"What's going on?" Emery asked, stairs creaking as he came down.

"Pops, Jem's teaching me how to pick someone's pocket!"

Emery's gaze swiveled from Colt to Jem. "Excuse me?"

Jem prided himself on being able to read the room. "You know what? We'll hang out upstairs."

3

"No," Tean said, adjusting the training treat in Evie's pudgy hand. "Don't let her have it yet."

The smell of liver wafted up. The puppy licked her lips. She shifted forward. She wriggled her tiny puppy hips.

"Tell her again," Tean said.

"She won't do it," Emery said. "I've barely been able to get that thing to stop pissing in the house."

"Go on," Tean said, one hand flat on the puppy's rear end, applying gentle pressure. "Tell her."

"Sit!" Evie commanded.

The puppy's legs folded slightly, her bottom dipping toward the floor but not quite making contact.

Evie squealed in delight and threw the treat at the dog. She scooped it up before Tean could recover it, and then she sprinted off. Evie laughed, and then, to Tean's surprise, she hugged him. A moment later, she was off again, chasing the puppy.

When Tean looked up, Emery was watching him with an unreadable look. A beat passed, and then Emery said, "Isn't that inconsistent? She didn't sit, but you still gave her the treat."

"She's learning."

"She's learning that a show of compliance will get her a reward."

"Ok," John-Henry said from where he was drying the dishes. "No more Kant at bedtime."

"It's obviously problematic—"

In the living room, out of sight of Emery and John-Henry, Jem was pretending to strangle himself with his t-shirt while Colt laughed into a pillow.

"What's her name?" Tean asked hurriedly.

Emery stared at him. Then, in two deliberate syllables, said, "Evie."

"Not her. The dog."

Emery made a sound of disgust.

John-Henry burst out laughing.

"I'm glad the chief of police finds it amusing," Emery said, "that his son would like to name the flea-infested—"

"I don't think she has fleas," Tean said.

"—mangy—"

"I definitely didn't notice mange."

"—mutt—"

"Actually, I believe she might be a purebred. She certainly looks like a—"

"Will you let me finish?"

It was not quite a shout, but Tean would have sworn the plates rattled inside the cabinets.

Jem was now dying on the floor, struggling so hard to be silent that his face was red.

"Uh, of course."

"Go ahead, Colt. Tell them what you wanted to name this…infestation."

Colt was wheezing into a pillow. Jem had tears streaming down his face.

"What is so funny?" Tean muttered. He looked for something to throw at his husband.

"Dank," Emery said.

Jem lost it. Croaking with laughter, he managed to get himself upright and stumble away.

"I'm sorry—" Tean began.

"Blitz, Blaze, Smoke, Spark, Fire. Colt Kimble Ballantyne, I can hear you laughing!"

Tean caught himself about to smile. John-Henry flashed him a grin; when Emery turned around, he ducked his head and pretended to be focused on drying the next dish.

"It will be a tremendous reassurance to the people of this city to know that their chosen representative of law and order finds it hilarious to name a dog using drug slang."

"Dank," Jem said from upstairs, followed by peals of laughter.

Emery's jaw tightened.

"I'm sure we can come up with a good name," Tean said. "A dog needs a name."

Evie and the puppy raced through the kitchen to stand in front of Tean. Evie held out one small hand, stuck out her tongue, and panted.

"Are you a puppy too?" Tean asked.

"She is not a puppy," Emery said.

Evie panted, tongue still lolling, and nodded.

"Do you want a treat?" Tean asked.

More panting. More nodding.

"No," Emery said, "she can't have those."

"What's your name, puppy?"

Evie forgot to pant as she considered that question.

"She's a human child—"

"Ree," John-Henry said, and Emery fell silent.

"Let me think," Tean said. "I can't give you a treat if I don't know your name. Is it Spud?"

Evie thought about that for a moment. Then she shook her head.

"Is it Mr. Waffles?"

Evie hesitated. Another no.

"Is it Tater?"

An emphatic shake of the head.

Tean pretended to consider the matter. "I think I've got it."

Evie bounced on her toes.

"Is it Biscuit?"

She panted, nodding her head enthusiastically.

"Here's your treat, Biscuit." Tean mimed giving her something, and Evie pretended to eat it. Then he said, "Does your friend want a treat too?"

All of a sudden, the game was over. Evie-the-puppy was Evie-the-girl again. She shook her head and said, "Her name is Biscuit, and she wants a treat."

Tean hid his smile as he passed her one of the training treats.

"Biscuit, sit!" Evie screamed.

Biscuit sat.

Evie hurled the treat at her, and a moment later, dog and girl were gone. Their hammering steps faded to silence. Colt was sitting up, a little goggle eyed now, and Jem perched at the top of the stairs, watching.

"Fuck me sideways," Emery breathed.

"She's, er, very assertive," Tean said.

John-Henry smirked. "Wonder who she got that from."

4

"Then cut your damn hair!" Emery shouted.

Colt loosed an animal noise of rage and stomped up the steps.

From the living room, Jem watched the teenager go.

Tean was in the backyard, training Biscuit—and, in the process, training Evie—while John-Henry and Jem watched *SportsCenter*. Emery had been reading a book until Colt had come downstairs with the sole purpose, it seemed, of picking a fight about his hair.

John-Henry didn't move. As far as Jem could tell, he didn't even breathe.

"Then you handle it next time," Emery said.

"I didn't say anything."

"He's right: it looks fucking ridiculous. What does he want me to say?" John-Henry rubbed one eye. "He wants you to—"

"He wants to grow out his hair like Ashley."

"His boyfriend," John-Henry said in an aside to Jem.

"That's irrelevant," Emery snapped. "All the articles say that if you want to grow your hair out, you have to be willing to deal with some awkward phases. We talked about this."

"I don't think he wants—"

"I explained it to him again. Right now."

"Ree," John-Henry said.

"Why is it my fault? What the fuck am I supposed to do about it?"

"Ok, ok." John-Henry swung bare feet down from the coffee table. "I'm going."

"What's that supposed to mean?"

"Don't let him change it to a documentary," John-Henry said, tossing the remote in Jem's lap. "It's my night to pick."

"We don't have nights. Nights imply a schedule, or a rotation, or a chart."

"He's gearing up." John-Henry's voice drifted back down the stairs. "Get ready."

SportsCenter wasn't exactly Jem's show, but he didn't mind it either. At home, they—meaning Tean—tried to limit screen time, including the TV. Gone were the days of watching six, eight, twelve hours of TV, until your eyeballs felt gummy and you had sugar build-up from Coke and Red Bulls between your teeth.

"Are you watching this?"

Jem's attention snapped back. "What? Oh no, he already warned me."

"Don't be ridiculous; John was joking. He's under a persistent delusion that he's a comedian."

"Right."

"If you're not watching it, there's no reason to leave it on."

"I might be watching it."

"What does that mean? You don't know if you're watching it? How is that even possible?"

"All things are possible to those who believe. I think I heard that in church once."

Emery's eyes narrowed.

Jem thought maybe the remote control would be safer tucked between his leg and the arm of the couch.

Then, from upstairs, came a scream of pure anguish: "Are you shitting me?"

"Jesus fucking Christ," Emery muttered, pushing his hands through his hair. "Language!"

"How old is he?"

"Sixteen going on thirty. I swear to God, this fucking hair thing is going to kill me."

Jem slid off the couch. He tucked the remote into the pocket of his shorts and headed for the stairs.

"You can leave that here," Emery said.

"Nice try."

In the cramped bedroom, Jem rooted around in his bag until he found the hair serum he wanted, the one he liked to use on Tean—when he could wrangle Tean into letting him. He had visions of one of those things they used at the dog groomers, the one that holds the dogs in place so they can't move. Only husband sized. Jem grabbed a few more supplies and ended up in the bathroom doorway for Act 3 of The Murdering of a Teenage Boy.

"Quit telling me how fucking handsome I am," Colt was shouting at John-Henry. "This is the stupidest fucking haircut I've ever seen."

Jem had known John-Henry for less than a week, but he was a good judge of people, and he thought John-Henry didn't get angry often. Right then, though, a vein was pulsing in John-Henry's temple, and red blotched the smooth gold of his complexion, and the muscles in his jaw looked like they were about to pop off the bone.

"I understand you're upset—" John-Henry began.

"Mind if I cut in?" Jem asked.

John-Henry shot him a look. Colt, teary eyed, tried for a watery glare. He wasn't wrong—John-Henry had done something like a businessman's side part, and it left Colt looking like a total wiener.

"Easy fix," Jem said. "Trust me."

"No—" Colt said, his voice thick.

"We're going to do a bit of a fade on the sides and back. Not much, just enough to even it out while it keeps growing. And then a little strategery, a few adjustments, some tricks up my sleeve, and you're going to look fire."

Colt rubbed his arm across his eyes. "Ok," he finally managed. "I guess."

"Are you kidding me?" John-Henry said. "When I said something was fire, you told me nobody says that anymore."

Colt sent him a dirty look.

"You said you'd rather die than be seen in public with me or Ree."

"That's because you're old," Colt said. "Jem's cool."

John-Henry opened his mouth, but nothing came out.

"I've got this," Jem said and nudged him out into the hall. "Wash your hair, and then we'll do the fade, and then I'll show you some options."

John-Henry put a hand on the jamb. "Jem, you don't have to—"

Jem waved a hand.

"Can you go, please?" Colt asked.

Jem cleared his throat.

"And, um, thank you. For trying. Even though it looked like shit."

"Close enough," Jem murmured.

When Colt's back was turned, John-Henry mouthed, *Thank you*, and then he disappeared down the stairs.

Colt ran water in the sink. Jem checked his clippers. He leaned against the wall as Colt worked the shampoo into his hair.

"So, who's Ashley?"

Who said teenagers were hard to talk to? After that, Jem couldn't get him to shut up.

5

Tean's vision of a relaxing, quiet evening was currently going up in flames.

"We probably shouldn't," Tean said.

Emery didn't seem to have heard him. It felt like a losing battle.

"Scratch that," Jem said. "We definitely shouldn't."

John-Henry had opted for shorts and an expensive-looking t-shirt; Tean didn't recognize the brand. Emery wore jeans and a black tee, and neither article of clothing did much to hide his body.

As he stepped into a sandal, John-Henry said, "We won't be gone long."

"How does twenty years sound?" Emery asked. "After they're both through puberty."

"Ha ha," Tean said.

For some reason, that cracked both of them up: a laugh from John-Henry, one of Emery's little smiles—albeit not so little right then.

"We might be—" Tean stalled. "We might be identity thieves."

"No worries," John-Henry said. "I'm taking my ID with me."

"For God's sake, John. It was one time; let it go." Emery held up a finger. "One time, once, in one single instance, a little gossamer flutter of a twink carded him, and he won't let it go."

"You're going to a bar," Tean said. "We love bars."

"It's more of a club."

"We love clubs."

Because Jem was a traitor, he laughed.

"We're not reputable," Tean tried. "We look disreputable."

"You look like you have a 401k," John-Henry said with a grin, and Jem burst out laughing again.

Emery perked up. "Is it diversified? What kind of plans do you have to choose from?"

"Surely you don't trust us with your children."

"Colt?" Emery called.

A slightly-less-shaggy head raised itself from the sofa long enough to say, "Jem's dope."

"Evie?"

She was bouncing, a blanket in one hand, Biscuit's collar in the other. "Mr. Tee, Mr. Tee, Mr. Tee."

"Oh my God," Jem said. "You are literally the new Mr. T. We need to get you chains. No, a mohawk. No, chains. No, both."

"I'm not literally the new anything," Tean snapped. "Why aren't you helping?"

Jem shrugged.

"You have a million excuses for everything."

"That doesn't sound like me."

"One time, when I asked you to vacuum the stairs, you told me you couldn't do it because Luke Perry died and you didn't know if you'd ever recover."

A laugh broke free from John-Henry.

Tean pointed at Jem. "He tried to stay in bed for two days."

"It was a hard time for all of us," John-Henry said, but he couldn't keep a straight face.

"Come on," Tean said, "do something."

"Um," Jem said, "I broke my ankle."

"No worries," John-Henry said. "You can just stay on the couch. Colt won't move for approximately sixteen hours."

Tean scowled at his husband.

"I'm one of those hobo drifters," Jem said. "I'm not to be trusted."

"A hot meal, a shower, and you can hit the road with your bindle in the morning."

"You're doing this on purpose," Tean said. "Remember when the gutters needed cleaning and you had that miraculous bout of sciatica?"

"It wasn't miraculous; it was agonizing."

"The fact that it disappeared after we got leaf guards installed was pretty miraculous!"

"We're strangers," Jem said. "You definitely shouldn't leave your kids with strangers."

John-Henry rolled his eyes.

Emery said, "He's not wrong, John. I've hired twelve-year-olds off the internet with better references than theirs."

"See?" Tean said. "Exactly."

"What twelve-year-olds?" Jem said. "Where? I'll beat them up."

Colt really loved that one, apparently.

"We might have medical conditions," Tean said. "We might be liable to pass out. We could lose consciousness, and then there would be no responsible adults."

"Colt's got a great head on his shoulders," John-Henry said. "He doesn't need a sitter, and he can help you if you need anything."

The look on Emery's face called that into question.

John-Henry continued, "Evie's obsessed with you. Biscuit is a ferocious guard dog. Noah and Rebeca are right next door, and in their free time, they're practically raising our children for us. And here's the important part: we trust you."

"Plus our usual sitters are busy," Emery said.

"What?" Tean asked, unable to keep the bitterness out of his voice. "Did they have a Girl Scout convention?"

"Yes."

There didn't seem to be much to say to that.

"Did we say thank you for doing this?" John-Henry asked.

"A thank you is irrelevant," Emery said. "They're freeloaders; they need to do their share of work around here."

John-Henry's grin hovered somewhere between amused and apologetic as he let himself out of the house.

After they'd left, Jem and Tean stood alone in the entry hall.

"Come on," Jem whispered. "It'll be fun. You're so good with kids."

Tean couldn't keep the look off his face.

"What?"

"It's just.. it's a lot of responsibility. And we barely know them. And—"

"And Evie is obsessed with you, and I swear to God, I've never seen Colt move so fast as when you asked him to help you with the Wi-Fi."

Tean nodded.

"How about this?" Jem asked. "You go upstairs and call the girls. Check in. Take a few minutes to be by yourself, relax. We'll switch in a little while."

Tean looked in the direction of the stairs. He thought of the chaos of the last week. He thought of the parade of people, the nonstop talking, the frenetic movement. He thought of an hour in a quiet room with a book. After calling the girls, of course.

"Are you sure?"

"Sure, I'm sure." The crooked front teeth flashed out with his grin. "We're a team."

Add Me Back

This story takes place before *The Girl in the Wind.*

1

Lana laughed as she went down the slide.

Theo waited nearby—not too close, under Lana's strict orders not to interfere. Not as close as he wanted, Auggie knew; if Theo had his way, he'd be in a catcher's stance at the bottom. But close enough. Evie ran circles on the pea-gravel fill while she waited for Lana so they could make their way to the top of the slide again.

Auggie, as usual, had been given the hardest job of all.

"What in the seven fucks is wrong with her?" Emery said. Then he looked at Auggie. "Well? You're the expert."

Auggie tried not to sigh.

Emery Hazard and his husband, John-Henry Somerset, were family friends, although Emery, in particular, had taken that label in new and interesting directions. Auggie's version of found family, for example, included only one person—so far—who had rifled their bookshelf and tossed every piece of fiction "post-Zola" into a cardboard box and ordered them to take the books to charity. That, er, boldness was currently manifesting again.

"Is it her crotch?" Emery asked before Auggie could answer. "Is her crotch the problem?"

Across the park, a woman was taking selfies. She was thirty going on thirteen, in a cropped tank top and jean shorts. The shorts were very short, and that was coming from Auggie, who owned —as Theo had once pointed out—shorts smaller than some of Theo's underwear. This woman's shorts were currently riding up so high they might as well have been on a voyage of no return. Her boyfriend or husband or partner or whatever, watching her from where he sat on a bench, couldn't seem to keep his hand out of his pants.

"I don't think anything's wrong with her," Auggie said.

"To Emery's point, though," John-Henry said, "those shorts can't be comfortable."

"That's putting it mildly," Emery said. "Is she having a stroke? A petit mal, perhaps."

"I think she'd know if she were having seizures," Auggie said.

"Maybe no one has ever asked before. Maybe everyone has always assumed that her behavior—" At that moment, the woman was arching her back, arm outstretched in search of some impossible angle that physiology wouldn't allow. "—is normal."

"Right, but—" Auggie stopped there.

John-Henry's smirk broadened.

Auggie gave him a pleading look.

John-Henry was many things. He was also, apparently, capable of being a tremendous shit while generating an aura of intense innocence.

"So," Emery said, "you can't explain. Isn't this your job?"

With a final dirty look for John-Henry, Auggie said, "No, I mean—look, lots of people like to take a lot of selfies. And then they go through them later, and they decide which ones they like, and they try some different filters, and they post their favorites. I mean, it's fun. It's kind of—"

John-Henry's eyes got wide, and he shook his head.

"—an art," Auggie finished.

"An art?" Hazard said.

"Uh, like maybe a new kind of—"

"Like Leonardo da Vinci, or Rembrandt, or Picasso."

"Well—"

"I suppose Seurat was experiencing extreme crotchal chafing from his booty shorts while he painted *La Grande Jatte*."

"To be fair," John-Henry put in, "he actually might have been suffering some crotch rot. Wasn't syphilis rampant back then?"

"We're not talking about syphilis," Emery snapped. "We're talking about—about that!"

"She's just trying to—" Auggie began.

The woman chose that moment, as she perched on the back of a bench in search of the perfect selfie, to tumble ass over teakettle.

Emery made a noise that sounded both disgusted and incredibly satisfied.

Then genius struck.

"You know what?" Auggie said. "You should be thinking about it differently."

"Good Lord, Auggie," John-Henry said under his breath. It was the same tone he might have used, Auggie guessed, if Auggie had announced his plans to go skydiving without a parachute.

"Excuse me?" Emery said.

"You should be thinking about it from an investigative angle."

"I'm perfectly capable—"

"I mean, the photos alone are valuable, right?" Auggie pulled out his phone to display it. "A lot of people leave their accounts public because, well, that's the whole point—they want attention, they want likes, they want responses. And so, everyone has access to them. And if you were trying to find this woman, like, say you were tracking her for—"

"Crotchal battery," John-Henry murmured.

Emery flashed him a look that rated at about an eight on Auggie's scale of terrifying. For some reason, though, it only made John-Henry smile.

"—um, whatever," Auggie powered through, "and you were looking at her account, you could see these pictures of the park and use them to make some educated guesses about where she lives, where she spends her time, that kind of thing."

Emery grunted.

"And it's more than that." Auggie held up his own phone in demonstration. "If you can get access to their account, you can learn all sorts of things about them from their ads. They're based on searches, interactions, all sorts of data that goes into an algorithm and decides what they see."

Something on Emery's face changed.

John-Henry glanced over and let out a strangled laugh.

Auggie suspected that somewhere, somehow, he had made a mistake.

"I suppose," Emery said, and it was hard to say what, exactly, was different, but he was smiling now, the smile so tiny it might have been invisible, "that explains the ads on your phone."

"No," Auggie said. Heat flashed into his face as he locked the phone and stuffed it into his pocket. "I do lots of research—"

"For example," Emery said, "a pair of low-rise briefs that say only 'Demon Twink.'"

"That's not—I'm not—I didn't—" One last-ditch effort: "It was the algorithm!"

"DILF Dungeon, Auggie?" John-Henry said as he started across the playground. "Really?"

2

The problem was this stupid video wasn't going to finish itself. Which was why Auggie was chained to his desk. Even though it was a beautiful day, and even though Lana was at an adventure camp, and even though it was, in theory, the perfect opportunity to do something fun and maybe even sexy with Theo, because Lord knew when the last time that had been. The other problem, of course, was that all the material Auggie had for the video—clips he was supposed to edit together for a social media campaign about pap smears—were, well…

"A disaster," Auggie said to the empty living room. "I've got a full-fledged disaster on my hands."

From the front of the house came the sound of a door opening, then footsteps.

"Thank God," Auggie said, dropping the tablet as he scrambled to his feet. "I know we said no funny business until I finished this video, but if I could just get off—"

He stopped because it wasn't Theo in the hall.

It was North McKinney and Shaw Aldrich. The two men were partners, in every sense of the word—romantically, professionally, and probably, a distant part of Auggie admitted, criminally. They were technically private investigators.

"We let ourselves in," Shaw announced with what sounded like pride.

"You were saying," North said with a grin.

"Get off this phone call," Auggie said.

North's grin didn't get bigger, but it glimmered in his eyes now.

"With a client."

"Uh huh."

"In my office. The phone is in my office."

"We thought you meant sex," Shaw said.

Auggie laughed. Too much. When he finally managed to stop himself, he asked, "What are you guys doing here?"

"Emery and John-Henry said we needed to have an adventure," Shaw said as he brushed past Auggie and continued into the house. From the living room, his voice floated back. "Oh, this is so pretty!" Which was followed by the unmistakable sound of something breaking.

"They kicked us out," North said, and when he passed Auggie, he didn't bump into him, and he didn't shoulder check him. He barreled toward him, on course for the kind of full-bodied collision that Fer had loved to do—still loved to do when he was being an asshole, which was ninety percent of the time. Auggie ducked out of the way, and for some reason, that made North laugh. He swatted at Auggie, and Auggie ducked that too. "Plus, we were bored."

"Ok, well—"

But North had already disappeared into the next room. "Huh." The words drifted back. "That was pretty."

"—I'm working," Auggie finished.

"I told you they were going to beat us here." That voice came from behind Auggie, and he spun around to see Jem and Tean entering through the still-open door. Jem gave Auggie a nod as he continued speaking to Tean. "That's why I was supposed to drive."

"You wanted to drive because you wanted to rev your engine at him when we stopped at that light." Tean looked around, frowned, and added, "Hi, Auggie."

"Yes, duh," Jem said, "revving your engine is the coolest part." He shouted down the length of the house, "That one didn't count, ass-weeds! Tean was driving."

"Is that reclaimed wood?" Tean asked.

"What are you doing here?" Auggie asked. He couldn't keep the despair out of his voice.

Tean cocked a look at him, like maybe he heard the unique sound of someone's entire career coming apart at the seams. Jem, however, sauntered down the hall.

"He wanted me and North to get him off," Shaw said. "But we said no. Not because we didn't want to, because, you know, Auggie is very handsome, maybe almost as handsome as North."

"He's not," North said. "He's got a face like a butt crack, but, like a butt crack with surgical-grade hemorrhoids."

"We didn't do it because of reasons." Shaw sounded like he was on less stable ground when he added, "Like, morality."

"And because Theo is one scary motherfucker," North muttered. Then, in a louder voice, "I didn't say that!"

"And Auggie had a phone call!" Shaw added triumphantly.

Maybe the panic showed on Auggie's face. Maybe Tean had some sixth sense for people who were in a soul-crushing vise of total defeat.

Tean's eyebrows drew together, and he frowned. "I'll get them out of here."

"Oh my God," Auggie whispered. "Thank you."

He followed Tean back to the living room. North had the fridge open and was considering Theo's selection of beers. Shaw had, apparently, only broken one thing so far—a vase that had come from Target, which, all things considered, wasn't a big deal. He was currently holding Auggie's tablet and tapping the screen with a worrying amount of interest. Jem was going through their mail and appeared to be considering a credit card offer.

"You've got a lot of files on here," Shaw said as he tapped the screen again. "You really need to clean this up."

"Please put that down," Auggie said. "That's for work."

"I think we should get out of here," Tean said. "Auggie—"

"Needs to get his rocks off," North said.

"He's waiting for Theo to—" Shaw jerked the air with one hand. "Only faster. Wait, Auggie, faster? Or slower? Or tighter? Is this too tight?"

"Don't mind us," Jem said as he picked up another piece of mail. "We'll be fine."

"We're going, that's what we're doing," Tean said.

"We just got here!"

"Jem, he's got things to do, and he's—"

"Backed up," North said as he spun the cap off a beer.

"That's serious," Shaw said. "His balls might explode."

"You have to go!" Auggie didn't even know the words were there until they'd left his mouth. He took a deep breath. "I'm sorry. I've got a million things to do, and we'd love to have you over another time, but right now, I've got to work."

Jem squared up a piece of mail on the counter. North ran his thumb along the mouth of the bottle. Shaw wrapped his hands around the tablet. Tean wiped his hands on his jeans.

Then a sound Auggie had never heard before came from the tablet. Shaw's whole body went still. Then he lifted his hands gingerly, peeling them away from the screen. He studied it. Then he smiled.

"I fixed it!" He displayed it to the room. "Look, all those messy files are gone!"

3

During the dinner rush, the seating at Cock of the Walk was at a premium. Like, bloodbath-level premium. So, Auggie and Tean grabbed a table while Jem and Theo stood in line to order. The restaurant—barely more than fast food, but some of the best fried chicken and biscuits in town—was full of bodies and voices and the smell of honey and cornmeal and, of course, the deep fryers and shimmering-hot oil.

"I'm sorry about your tablet," Tean said.

Auggie waved a hand. "It's ok—I have the raw videos backed up, and everything I'd done today was crap anyway."

"Still, you worked hard, and I'm sorry. We shouldn't have interrupted."

"It's hard to be mad at Shaw. He's like a little kid sometimes."

"He does seem…" Tean drew back from finishing the sentence.

"Touched?" Auggie asked dryly.

A quiet laugh rippled out from Tean. "I was going to say innocent, but yeah, touched. A little."

"He's apparently very good at what he does, whatever that is. Drive North crazy, I guess."

That made Tean laugh again.

Silence fell between them, which was strange, because a red-faced white guy on Auggie's left was shouting into his phone, "This is our chance! This is our chance!" and on Auggie's right, two teenage boys were screaming in each other's faces about who got the last biscuit, their voices pitching more and more sharply until they both dissolved into laughter.

If the lull in the conversation bothered Tean, he didn't show it. He sat with his back straight, his hands on his thighs. His gaze moved around the room, and when it came back to Auggie and he saw Auggie watching him, he smiled: small, a hint of lines in his forehead.

"I'm sorry. I'm not very good at this."

Auggie blinked. "Good at what?"

"Uh—" That uncertain smile came again. "Take your pick."

For some reason, that made Auggie laugh, and some of the stiffness in Tean's back eased.

"Usually, Jem is the one who, you know, talks to people. I don't mind talking, but it's easier when Jem does it."

Over Tean's shoulder, Auggie watched Jem and Theo in line. Jem said something, and Theo laughed and pushed back his bro flow of strawberry-blond hair, the movement unconscious and automatic and so wonderfully Theo that, for a moment, Auggie's chest was tight. But he watched a moment longer, wondering. He'd taken a lot of photos. He'd looked at, and watched, a lot of people. He knew how he'd frame the shot of Theo and Jem. And he knew, if he were giving instructions, he'd tell Theo to angle his body more toward Jem. He'd say something about taking his hands out of his pockets. He'd say, *Smile with your eyes.*

"Is something wrong?" Tean twisted to look over his shoulder. As though sensing the attention, Jem glanced back and waved, and Theo gave Auggie a crooked smile—a little rueful, a little wry.

"Theo's starting to like Jem," Auggie said as Tean settled into his seat again. "And he's trying to pretend he's not because he's Theo and he's determined to be serious and responsible, but there's this wild part of him that he can't quite outgrow."

Tean's quiet laugh was a little fuller this time. "That sounds familiar."

"How long have you and Jem been together?"

"A couple of years. Kind of. We had a rocky start."

Auggie's grin slipped out. "You too?"

"Pretty bad." But amusement lurked in the words. "You?"

"God, almost seven, but like you said, only kind of. Theo was my professor."

For a moment, Tean's jaw loosened. When Auggie burst out laughing, Tean said, "No, no, no. I'm sorry! I didn't mean—it's just, he doesn't look— you're not—"

Auggie laughed harder.

Shrinking down into his seat, Tean shook his head. "Never mind. I'm done. I'm officially done talking."

"No, it's fine. I promise, it's completely fine. I kind of like telling people. You never know what kind of reaction you're going to get."

Tean shook his head and mimed zipping his lips.

Relaxing back into the chair, Auggie studied the other man. The line in Tean's forehead was deeper, and he was still giving tiny shakes of his head. After a moment, fighting a smile, Auggie said, "You're a vet, right?"

Tean nodded.

"Do you like it?"

Another nod.

"Are you really not going to talk?"

"Not until Jem gets back." But then he rolled his eyes, blew out a breath, and said, "You do social media stuff?"

"Yep."

"What does that mean? I asked, and nobody seemed to know. And I don't know anything about social media except for this stupid dating app Jem made me get once, and oh my God, why am I still talking?"

"That's all right; I'm glad you asked. It's hilarious, sometimes, watching people try to figure it out. But sometimes it's annoying. I do a lot of stuff, actually. I used to do a lot of original content, funny videos, that kind of thing. I still do one every once in a while, but mostly I run what's essentially a boutique digital marketing agency. I like to say boutique because it's better than one-man or self-employed or even freelancer. I help with marketing campaigns, I curate influencers, I do some video and photo editing, although not as much anymore. Whatever a client needs, basically."

"Theo says you're very successful. He didn't say it like that, of course, but that was the message."

In the line for the register, Theo had his head bent, listening to whatever Jem was saying.

"Theo is very kind," Auggie said.

"He's also very proud of you."

It was like sunlight spilling through a window. "I think he is. Most of the time."

Tean smiled, and then another of those breaks came in the conversation. Tean straightened the napkin holder, the salt and pepper shakers, the ketchup, and the tray with the sweetener packets. The guy on Auggie's left had given up on his phone now and was going ham on a drumstick, his breathing labored between the smack of lips and the knocking sound of his teeth against bone. One of the biscuit boys was slumped in the booth and playing on his phone, a foot kicked up on the table and resting among their trash; the other boy had disappeared.

"So, you've never used Facebook?" Auggie asked. "Or Instagram, or Twitter, or Snapchat, or TikTok—wait, what about Myspace? Are you even old enough for a Myspace? Theo refuses to tell me what he had on his page."

"Uh, definitely no Myspace."

"How about Instagram? Instagram is a great one to start with." Auggie slipped into the seat next to Tean. "Have you ever used it?"

Tean shook his head. "Hannah—a friend—keeps telling me to get it. Apparently there are some good wildlife accounts, but..."

"It's super easy. Look, here's mine. The whole point is to share pictures." Tean's expression changed, and Auggie said, "You don't have to do pictures of yourself, although that's what a lot of people do. You can just post about your animals, or your kids, or your trips. I like to do stuff from daily life because I like having a record, if that makes sense. Kind of documenting my life—but for me. Like this."

He leaned back, an arm around Tean, and held up the camera. Tean's shoulders were stiff, and his smile looked more like a grimace, but Auggie snapped the picture anyway. He tweaked it with a filter and posted it with the rooster emoji and the word *bros*.

A comment appeared almost immediately, and Auggie locked his screen.

"What happened?" Tean asked.

"Oh. Nothing."

"It looked like someone said something. Like a comment."

"Oh." That didn't sound nearly as good the second time. "Huh. I'll have to—there you guys are!"

Theo quirked an eyebrow at the greeting.

"Did you see the line?" Jem asked as he and Auggie traded spots. "People are crazy about this place."

"Everything ok?" Theo asked in a murmur.

Auggie made an OK sign with one hand below the table.

"Really?" Theo whispered. "Because I know you love the food here, but you don't normally shout, 'There you are' when I come back."

"Later," Auggie whispered back.

"Holy shit," Jem said. He stared at his phone and then burst out laughing.

"What?" Tean asked.

Jem laughed harder.

Auggie shook his head and tried to catch Jem's eye.

"Auggie?" Theo asked.

"Probably something random," Auggie said. "Right, Jem?"

Jem showed his phone to Tean. Tean stared and put his face in his hands. Still laughing, Jem turned the phone toward Theo. "Oh my God, Theo, look at this."

And there it was, the first comment still visible at the top as likes and responses piled up.

OMG u and ur dad r so cute!!!!

4

"That's it," Auggie said. "I'm done. The end."

He was trying to find new ways to say it; he'd used up most of his options on the ride home.

"It's fine," Theo said. Theo, in contrast, wasn't trying to find new ways of saying anything. He'd told Auggie it was fine approximately a million times on the short drive.

"Did you see his face?"

"I did."

"Would you call that a happy face?"

The tires thrummed.

"See?"

"I think he was surprised."

"Theo!"

"Auggie, I don't know what to tell you. He's got to be fifteen years older than you. The glasses make him look even older."

The leaves of the silver maples glinted in the headlights.

"Are you saying what I think you're saying?" Auggie asked.

Theo seemed to think about that and then, in that judicious Theo tone, said, "No."

"I think you are."

"Auggie."

"Do you think we look like we could be father and son?"

"Did you ever hear the old piece of advice, 'Don't ask questions you don't want to know the answer to'?"

It was hard to talk when the bedrock of your life was betraying you, but a moment later, Auggie managed a strangled "What?"

Theo wasn't smiling as he parked in front of their front door. Not exactly.

The house was quiet. Lana was in bed already, and from the back of the house, where Auggie might have expected the sound of the TV, he heard nothing. And then he heard something. Something familiar.

"Loud steps," Auggie said.

Theo rolled his eyes, but he did walk a little more heavily than usual, and before they reached the family room, he called, "We're home."

Not loud enough to wake Lana, but loud enough to be heard over…other things.

When they stepped into the family room, Colt was sitting up, his face flushed, trying to fix his hair. His lips were puffy. Ashley, his boyfriend, took the opposite route: he was apparently determined to find a secret door at the bottom of the sofa, and he was making himself smaller and smaller—and trying to pull a pillow over his lap—in search of that magical exit.

"Uh, hey, Dr. Stratford," Colt managed.

"Hey."

Auggie gave him a dirty look and then asked the boys, "Everything went ok?"

"Oh yeah," Colt said. "Lana's obsessed with Ash."

"That makes two of you," Theo said, but because he was Theo, not loud enough for Colt to hear. In a stronger voice, he added, "Thanks for doing this. Let me just check on Lana, and you guys can go."

"We'll just sit right here," Ashley blurted, crossing his arms over the pillow.

Theo did roll his eyes, but only a little.

"Did you guys have a nice night?" Auggie asked as Theo's steps moved off.

Colt snickered. Ashley's face turned even redder. The pillow would have to go, Auggie decided. There was no way to save it, not at this point.

"Um, yeah," Colt said. "Really nice."

This time, both of them giggled.

When Theo got back, he said, "Sound asleep. You guys are probably tired, so you can head home."

"Nah," Colt said. "We're just getting started." He must have heard how that sounded because his eyes widened, and more of that color rushed back into his face.

"They're young," Auggie said. "They're not old and decrepit like us."

"Nice try," Theo said.

"You guys aren't old," Colt said, but it sounded like loyalty talking. "My dads are old."

"Yeah, Mr. Lopez," Ashley said stoutly. "Thirty isn't old."

A quiver went through Theo, and he covered his mouth and turned and walked away. Fast.

Betrayal on every side, Auggie thought. And then, the way a prizefighter might feel after getting his bell rung, Thirty?

"Stay there for a second," Auggie said, wondering if the words sounded as dazed as they felt. He made his way to Theo in the kitchen, where Theo was uncapping a beer. His lips were twitching suspiciously.

"Are you holding those boys hostage?" Theo finally asked, and it sounded like his voice was slipping.

"Did you hear what that little shit just said to me?"

"I'm certainly hearing something right now."

"Was I like that when I was their age?"

"I didn't know you when you were their age," Theo said. And then, in an underbreath, he added, "Barely."

"Theo!" It was a whisper. But it was also a scream.

"I don't know what you're upset about. You don't want to look like Tean's son; fine, you're way more handsome than he is, and you don't look like a child. Ash tells you that you look great for thirty—"

"He didn't say that! He didn't say great!"

Theo sipped the beer for a suspiciously long time. Lowering the bottle, he continued, "—and to me, that says you look like an attractive, mature, adult male. You can't be mad about both things, Auggie. It's illogical."

"I can be mad about whatever I want!"

Maybe, a distant part of Auggie thought, maybe things were getting a little out of control, because he wasn't sure he'd ever seen that much white in Theo's eyes.

"And don't think," Auggie said in a vicious whisper, "I didn't notice that you avoided my question about how I acted when I was their age."

Theo eyed him over the mouth of the bottle. "Uh, I plead the Fifth? Auggie, come back, I'm teasing. You were very mature—"

Auggie rounded on him, a finger in Theo's face. "Now I have to go back over there. Now I have to prove it."

"Prove what?"

"I don't know!"

He hurried back to where Ashley and Colt had gotten to their feet. The boys were both looking at Ashley's phone, laughing softly, and then Colt said, "Oh my God, she's so cheugy."

"What does that mean?" Auggie asked, pulling out his phone. "Is that something I could use in a video?"

Ashley looked at Colt. Colt looked at Ashley.

"Go on, Ashley," Theo said from the kitchen. "You wrote a definition paper about it for me. Explain to Auggie what cheugy means."

It was hard to tell in the dim lighting, but it looked like Ashley lost a little color. "Um. Uh. It means, like, someone who's, you know—" He broke off—or maybe it was terror, a small voice in Auggie's head suggested, because Ashley was giving Auggie some very worried looks.

Colt jumped in. "It means, like, a millennial. You know, like you."

After the silence, Theo's laughter was shockingly evil.

Auggie's brain compartmentalized. He could deal with that particular problem—and that new treachery—later. He had to regroup. He had to prove—Theo's question floated again—something. That he was young sounded ridiculous, because he was young, felt young, knew he was young.

Cool, maybe. Did they even say cool? Could he be the son of a wildlife veterinarian and also be an aging millennial at the same time? It was like his life had taken a sharp and sudden turn, and he didn't recognize the route he was on.

Hair, part of his brain suggested. No, music. But then a tidal wave of horror rose in Auggie at the possibility of hearing the phrase "dad rock," and he shrank away from music. Clothes. He'd always dressed well. Kept up with the latest fashion. He had an eye for it, and almost as importantly, an eye for what looked good on other people.

"Hey, guys, before you go," Auggie said, the words spilling out too fast. "Theo and I were about to send some clothes to Goodwill—"

"We were?" Theo asked.

"—and I was wondering if you wanted to take a look through them. Some of Theo's stuff would fit you, and it's all new. It would look good on you."

Another of those breaks came in the flow of words. Apparently, it was agonizing enough to kill even Ashley's boner, because he tossed the pillow on the couch.

"Oh," he finally said. "Thanks, Mr. Lopez. I'm good."

"Did you see Mr. Berger's drip?" Colt said to Ashley. "That Nick at Night shirt is fu—freaking fire."

Drip, Auggie thought from a long way off. Remember to look up drip.

The boys shuffled toward the door, Auggie and Theo already forgotten.

"Old clothes are so dope," Ashley said, the words floating back from the front door.

"Yeah," Colt said, "I wish I was born in the Nineties."

5

Auggie pulled the covers over his head.

It was a gesture in show only; even though Lana was sitting next to him in bed, she was too busy with her cartoons to pay any attention to him, and there was zero chance of going back to sleep, and Theo was in the kitchen, so he couldn't even appreciate the drama of it.

Would a kid today say drama? Would they say something else? Was it cheugy to say drama? Oh God, was it cheugy to worry about being cheugy?

It had been a long night of fractured sleep and splintered dreams. That was to be expected when your life ended in a spectacular toilet-shaped fireball.

On the TV, someone was singing. A child. You're going to get old too. Auggie sent the thought toward the voice. You're going to get old, and one day a couple of horny teenagers are going to shove it in your face. Let's see how you like it.

Floorboards creaked. Steps moved toward the bedroom. A moment later, the door inched open, and the smell of carbs—big, fluffy, buttery carbs—wafted to Auggie. The mattress sank under new weight, and Theo's hand came to rest on Auggie's leg.

"I'm dead."

Theo sighed.

"I can't eat Big Biscuit because my ancient, desiccated, withered body—"

"Aren't withered and desiccated pretty much the same thing?"

Auggie threw back the covers and sat up.

"Ok," Theo said, holding up his free hand in surrender. "Go on."

"My ancient, desiccated, withered body," Auggie emphasized each word, "can't process anything delicious like Big Biscuit. Just get me some porridge. Or oatmeal. No, porridge would be better. I should have porridge. And throw away all my moisturizers; I'm going to give up and look like John-Henry with crow's feet. And I'm going to complain about music. And kids these days. And I'm going to wear black, knee-high socks with sandals."

"Are you done?"

"No. Do we own a VCR? And what channel is C-SPAN? Isn't there a C-SPAN2?"

Theo adjusted the rolled top of the takeout bag. The paper crinkled. He wore a partial smile, a little wrinkle between his eyebrows. "What's going on, sweetheart? You aren't upset about those boys. You tell me all the time you're glad you're not that age anymore. For God's sake, I think Ashley penetrated that pillow."

"Non-consensually, for the record."

"I'll put it in the report." Theo cocked his head. "The thing with Tean was a little embarrassing, but I think more for him; I mean, Auggie, people would kill to look like you. I'm not just talking about how handsome you are. You're going to get sick of people telling you this, but you're going to be glad you look young when you're—"

"Thirty?" Auggie said.

The angle of Theo's head became a little more...severe. "When you're forty, and when you're fifty, and on and on, you're going to be glad you look young."

"You're right: I'm sick of people telling me that."

Shifting his weight toward the edge of the bed, Theo said, "All right; we can have this conversation later."

"No! I'm sorry!" Auggie wrestled with his pride for longer than he would have liked, and then he was able to ask, "Did you get the cinnamon one?"

Theo relaxed back onto the mattress and opened the bag. The "cinnamon one" was in its own takeout container, an enormous biscuit drenched in butter and cinnamon brown sugar. Theo produced a fork like someone doing a magic trick, and Auggie speared some carbs. He chewed. He ate. Sugar hit his system like jet fuel, and when he looked at Theo again, he couldn't help the embarrassed smile.

Theo rubbed his leg. "Want to tell me what's going on?"

"I don't know, Theo. I mean, last night wasn't ideal. I was already fragile from being mistaken for Tean's son. Good Christ, I thought he was going to die."

A grin broke out on Theo's face. "He did not look happy."

"And I'd had that weird couple of days with Shaw deleting everything and Emery—" He cut himself off.

"What did Emery say to you?"

"Knock it off," Auggie said, but gently. "I don't need you to beat him up for me. He wasn't mean or anything. It's just been...a lot. And everything we went through last weekend—" Everything was a small way of describing the search for a two-time killer. "—and you guys are all so capable and competent and have real skills, even Tean, and I'm supposed to be good at one thing, and the last couple days are the full and total proof I'm not even good at that."

Theo pulled his legs up to sit crisscross. He took the takeout container, ignoring Auggie's whimper of protest, and pulled it away. Then he held Auggie's hands in his and squeezed them once. The eye contact was a lot, and after a moment, Auggie blinked and looked away. Lana must have sensed it because she leaned into him, and he snuffled and hugged her against him. She didn't stop watching her show, of course; total emotional devastation wasn't enough cause for that.

"You're good at so many things," Theo said, "and a couple of off days don't mean anything. And if those assholes—"

Auggie covered Lana's ear, pulling her head to his chest.

"If those jerks can't see it, it's their fault. You don't have anything to prove to them."

"I know."

"You certainly don't have to impress them."

"I know."

"You're smart and resourceful, and you know how to handle yourself when things get dicey."

Auggie looked at the ceiling.

Chuffing a laugh, Theo squeezed the hand he still held. "And if I wanted a street brawler, I would have gone out with Orlando."

Auggie's eyes snapped down. "Rude!"

He was going to say more, but his phone buzzed on the nightstand. He checked it. Then he frowned. Emery's name showed on the screen.

When Auggie answered on speaker, Emery was already talking. " — your ass over here and show me how to delete these."

"Hi, Emery."

"Auggie—" John-Henry spoke in the background. "—it's not a big deal. Enjoy your day off and ignore him."

"I'm sorry, John, but it's a big deal to me that a group of — of voyeurs and peeping Toms is circulating indecent photos of you on the internet."

Auggie blinked. Theo looked like he was trying not to laugh.

"John-Henry, are people posting thirst tweets about you?"

The sigh carried over the call. "I took my shirt off during this stupid five-K."

"To repeat," Emery said, "get your ass over here!"

"Uh, yeah," Auggie said, exchanging a what-do-I-do look with Theo. "I'll be over in a bit."

When he disconnected the call, Theo arched his eyebrows.

"That doesn't mean—" Auggie began.

But his phone rang again.

"I got hijacked," Shaw announced.

"You're not a fucking pirate ship," North shouted in the background. "You can't get hijacked."

"But it's ok. It's not my butt. It's my armpit."

"Uh."

"Can you please get over here," North bellowed, "and take this fucking spyware off his phone?"

In a whisper, Shaw added, "It might be North's butt."

"Right—" Auggie tried.

"It's my what?" North shouted, and then the call cut off.

The phone rang immediately.

Auggie eyed Tean's name. He looked at Theo. "Doesn't anyone know about texts?"

Theo swiped to answer the call.

"You've got to help me," Tean said.

"Yes, son," Jem said in the background. "Come help your aging father." Then he grunted like someone had elbowed him.

"Somehow my Prowler account turned on again, and there's a nude, and people won't stop texting me."

"It's not a nude," Jem wheezed. "He's wearing board shorts."

"I've got twenty-three male members in my inbox!" Tean said, voice unraveling with each word.

"I'll be right there?" Auggie said, unable to keep the question out of the words.

But when the call cut off, and Theo was fighting a grin, Auggie said, "I changed my mind. Colt and Ashley can help them; young people are good with technology."

Theo rolled his eyes.

And then a text came through: *What am I doing wrong?* And then a series of poorly composed selfies of Colt came through. *Is it my phone? My phone is broken.*

"You were saying?" Theo murmured.

Auggie grabbed the cinnamon biscuit and forked another mouthful as he wriggled out of bed. "I guess I should—I mean, if they need help."

"Actually, one thing," Theo said, pushing back his hair with both hands. "Before you go, uh, I think Lana deleted all my apps again."

Adulting is Hard

This story is set before *The Spoil of Beasts.*

1

"It's fine," Colt said. The teenager kept glancing at North and looking away again, shaking the keys to the Mustang in one loose fist. "J-H said I could borrow his car."

"Did he say you could borrow it?" Shaw asked. "Or did he say you could race North?"

"He said Colt could use it," North said. "That's what matters."

"Actually—" Shaw tried.

The stretch of empty country road shimmered under the August sun, and the muggy heat wrapped itself around everything.

"Come on," Colt said, wiping sweat from his forehead. "It's hot as balls out here."

"I don't think your dads would like you saying hot as balls."

"Are you kidding? Pops says way worse stuff. In front of Evie, too. J-H and I talk about it all the time."

"I just don't think it's safe—" Shaw said.

"Colt's right," North said. "It's hot as balls out here. I want to hand this kid and his pretty-boy car their collective asses, and then I want to go home. And drink a beer."

Colt laughed a little too hard. Then he jeered a little too emphatically. "It's going to be fun, watching the dinosaurs in my rearview mirror. Hey, North, remind me again—what's the horsepower on a 1968 GTO?"

"It's not all about horsepower, smartass."

"And what kind of traction control system do you have?"

"Get in your car, wise guy."

Colt laughed again as he jogged toward the Mustang.

When North turned toward the GTO, Shaw caught his sleeve. "You need to be careful with him, North."

North gave Shaw a long look, and then he said, "I've got it under control."

"I don't think you do. You should see how he looks at you when he thinks you're not paying attention."

"He likes to talk to me, that's all."

"That's not all. And he's got a boyfriend."

"Yeah, well, I'm not exactly a threat, am I?"

"No, but did you consider that Emery might murder you if he learns you're drag racing with his son?"

"That's why we're not going to tell him," North said as he pulled his arm free.

When Shaw got into the passenger seat, North groaned.

"What?" Shaw asked.

"We're racing."

"I know. It's exciting. I want to be part of it. And if we crash, I'll be thrown clear, and I can pull your mangled body from the fiery wreckage."

"Wouldn't that be nice?" North muttered.

"What?"

"You know you're dead weight, right? You can't have dead weight in a race."

"I'm not dead weight. I'm your navigator."

"Navi—it's a straight road!"

Colt honked his horn and then buzzed a window down. "What's wrong? Car won't start?"

"This fucking kid," North said under his breath.

"Do they still make leaded gasoline? Is that what it needs?"

"All right, all right, smartass," North said as he keyed the ignition. The GTO woke with a rumble, and North slouched back in the seat, checking gauges. The white tee clung to his chest where sweat dampened it. Muscles popped out along his arm as he checked the gear shift. Shaw tried to remind himself, forcibly, of all the reasons he didn't like muscle cars and the guys who drove them. The environment. Probably. It probably had something to do with the environment.

"It's not exactly tradition for the starter to be inside the car," North said, "but if you don't mind?"

Shaw counted them down. With a growl, the GTO lunged forward.

The Mustang was faster off the mark, though, and began to pull ahead. North swore as he shifted, and second by second, they began to close the gap. The straight stretch of road was shrinking toward a curve around the bluffs, and Shaw had a vision of a semi coming around the corner.

Then he saw the dog.

"Dog! North, stop!"

Another streak of swears blistered the air as North shifted and braked, and the GTO came to a halt with the screech of tires and the stink of burning rubber.

"Oh my God," Shaw said with a laugh, pushing hair out of his eyes. "It was just a rock."

North's breathing took on a...quality.

"Isn't that lucky, North?"

Ahead of them, Colt slowed and swung around. He braked when he pulled up next to them, a huge grin splitting his face. "Gas is on the right."

"Fucking kids these days," North said. "That one didn't count; Shaw distracted me."

The teenager was giggling as he accelerated back toward their improvised starting line.

"North," Shaw said.

"God damn it," North said. "I know."

When they got back to the starting line, Shaw did the countdown again. This time, Colt fumbled the start, and the GTO ate up the asphalt. The Mustang was clearly a car in a different league, with features and engineering fifty years newer than North's baby. But North had experience that Colt didn't. and on top of that, he was good at what he did. He had good hands, Shaw thought, watching those strong fingers wrap and re-wrap around the shifter. Strong, capable, skillful hands —

"Fuck, fuck, fuck, fuck!" North's swears escalated in volume, and Shaw glanced up. An ancient VW bus was coming around the corner ahead of them. North hit the brakes again, and they squealed to another stop.

Colt, of course, blew past them.

The VW's tired horn blatted at them, and as it passed the GTO, the driver—a shrunken man with a monk's ring of white hair—flipped them the bird.

"Fuck you, you gnarly old fuck," North shouted back.

"Language," Shaw murmured as Colt pulled up alongside them again.

"Do over," North said. "That was a fucking fluke."

"Language," Shaw tried again.

"I'll give you a head start," Colt said as he eased away from them. "Will five seconds be enough?"

"What the fuck is wrong with this world?" North said as they drove back to the starting line. "Do you hear how that kid talks to his fucking elders?"

"Maybe you do need—what was it called? A traction system?"

"I do not need a traction system. I need to get rid of this dead weight—"

"Hey!"

"—and I need one mile of uninterrupted road so I can hand that teenage smartass his—"

"Ass?"

North growled and slammed the brakes so hard, Shaw rocked forward in his seat.

"Third time's the charm," Colt said as they pulled up to the starting. "Don't worry, Gramps. You got this."

"Fucking son of a cocksucker," North muttered.

"What was that?" Colt called.

"Nothing! Shaw, start the fucking race."

Shaw counted them down.

Colt was first off the mark again, but North, swearing and muttering and grunting, closed the distance inch by inch. They caught up to the Mustang's rear bumper. Then they were half a car's length behind. Then they were neck and neck.

That was when the Wahredua PD cruiser came around the corner ahead of them, lights flashing.

"Aww, shit," North said.

This time, they had enough time and distance for a more graceful stop. The cruiser turned to block the road.

"Asshole," North said.

"North."

"What? That's a dick move."

Then the door opened, and John-Henry got out.

Shaw groaned and slumped in his seat.

"Hello, Colt," John-Henry said. "Hello, North. Shaw." His smile was a knife. "Why don't you all get out of your cars?"

2

North was considering a beer run to the kitchen, but he stopped in the opening that connected to the living room.

"And that," Shaw was saying to Emery, who was washing dishes, "is why North is more of an alpha male than a sigma male." Shaw laughed. "Oh my God, Emery, I got it backwards again. That's why North is more of a sigma male. Sigma. Like sigmoid colon. That's how I'm going to remember it."

How North was going to remember it, he thought, was by the look on Emery's face. Like he wanted to kill himself. Or kill Shaw and then himself. Or maybe just kill everyone.

But that still didn't settle the question of the beer. He inched into the kitchen and slid along the front of the refrigerator, trying to minimize his profile.

"On the other hand," Shaw said, "if we wanted to compare North's alpha qualities to his beta qualities—"

"I don't want to," Emery said.

"What?"

"I don't want to compare them. I don't want to continue this conversation. I don't want to do any of this."

"Oh," Shaw said.

North opened the fridge. He'd brought a couple of six-packs of Four Hands, and—yes, there was still one left.

"But in theory if we wanted to," Shaw said, "we could begin by talking about North's grooming habits. So, for example—wait, first I have to ask a question. When you take a shower, do you shower like a normal person and rub the soap on your skin? Or do you just work up a lather and then wipe your hands over your body? Or are you really mean like North sometimes and you use one corner of the soap like a shank and pretend to shank me like it's a prison shower, only then the other thing that happens in prison showers starts to happen, and North is all soapy and slippery—"

"Shaw!" North barked. Since the subterfuge was over, he went ahead and grabbed the last beer and slammed the fridge door.

"North! Oh my God, I was just telling Emery about that game we play—"

"Get him out of here," Emery said.

"For fuck's sake," North said, catching Shaw's arm. "Why is he my responsibility?"

When he released Shaw in the living room, Shaw immediately drifted over to Auggie. The younger man was lying on the floor, head propped on a pillow as he scrolled on his phone.

"Hi, Auggie," Shaw said.

Auggie made a noise that might have passed for greeting.

"I was just telling Emery all about North's alpha qualities versus his beta qualities—"

A little too quickly, Auggie said, "Oh gosh, I'm getting sleepy," and shut his eyes.

"Boy, you got tired fast," Shaw said. "You know what you should do? Auggie. Hey, Auggie. You know what you should do? You know what you and Theo should do?"

Auggie's eyes snapped open. "What?"

For a pipsqueak, North had to admit, he did have a pair of lungs on him.

"You should sun your perineums—perinea—North, what's the plural of perineum? Wait, Auggie, come back, it's the equivalent of a cup of coffee!"

When Shaw got up to follow Auggie, North said, "No."

"We were having a conversation—"

"Go bother someone else."

"I wasn't bothering him," Shaw said, but he said it in that way that made North extremely suspicious. Because sometimes, now, he couldn't tell how much of it was an act.

North cracked open his beer, slurped the foam from his knuckles, and prepared for a full intervention.

Thankfully, Shaw found his next victim quickly. Tean and Theo sat by the window. Theo had a birding book open on his lap, and Tean was looking through a pair of binoculars. As he passed the binoculars back to Theo, he said, "Take a look at that cherry tree near the top. I think that's a—"

"Are you guys looking at birds?" Shaw asked. "Because I love looking at birds."

The silence lasted a beat too long.

"Uh, yes—" Theo began.

"Did you know—oh, Tean, you're going to find this interesting—"

"I doubt that," North said.

Shaw cast him a furious look. "Did you know that in October of 2017, I was given the gift of speaking to birds? But I could only do it to some birds. And only through whistling."

"An entire fucking month," North said. "For the first two weeks, I thought I had tinnitus."

"If you'd like, I could see if I still have any of the ability left. What is that? What are we looking at?" Shaw climbed onto the sofa and wedged himself between them—in the process, knocking Tean's glasses askew and kicking Theo's birding book onto the floor. "Oh, great, a blue jay. I still know some blue jay—"

"Actually—" Tean straightened his glasses. "That's a blackbird."

"That's what I meant, blackbird."

"I'm sorry, Shaw, but would you mind—"

"Oh dang," Shaw said. "He flew away. Maybe next time!"

And with that, he scrambled down—this time, he managed to kick over Tean's Pepsi and step directly on Theo's foot.

John-Henry was next in the line of fire, and North took a long drink of his beer. John-Henry sat in front of a Bluetooth speaker, looking through music on his phone. Shaw plopped down next to him and, before John-Henry could protest, took the phone from his hand.

"Oh my God, John-Henry, I know the perfect thing for right now. Have you ever heard Tibetan throat singing? You're going to love it. Emery! John-Henry's going to love Tibetan throat singing!"

"Evie's asleep, you jackass!" Emery shouted back, which North had to admit, undercut the message a little.

Shaw hit play, and music began. North wasn't sure if he'd ever heard Tibetan throat singing before (it was probably one of those things that had happened to him and, like all trauma, he'd repressed it), but whatever this was, it was loud.

Upstairs, Evie began to cry.

John-Henry yanked his phone back, and the music cut off.

Emery appeared in the opening to the kitchen. He snapped a dishtowel tight between his hands, and his voice was strained as he said, "North."

Sighing, North finished the beer. "Come on."

"Where are you guys going?" Shaw asked.

"We're going," North said, grabbing Shaw's arm. "We. Outside."

From the foyer, Jem said, "Maybe you can still talk to that bluebird."

3

"No," North said and dropped onto the sofa.

"Please?"

North tried to ignore that, but Shaw moved into his line of sight — and, in the process, blocked the TV. North clicked the remote a few times, but nothing.

"It doesn't work on people," Shaw told him.

"Unfortunately."

"I'll do everything you say. I'll be so quiet and so obedient and so, um, submissive."

"This is taking an interesting turn," Jem said, looking up from his Goosebumps books.

North scowled at him. Then, to Shaw, he said, "Why? Why this sudden interest in lifting weights?"

"Because," Shaw said, "I'm going to be a muscle otter."

In the kitchen, John-Henry choked on something. For one shining, vicious moment, North hoped it was a chicken bone.

"What the fuck are you talking about, you're going to be a muscle otter?"

"A muscle otter is an otter who's got muscles —"

"I know what a muscle otter is. Anyone with two fucking brain cells knows what a muscle otter is."

Jem raised his hand. "I don't. Could you explain, maybe with diagrams?"

Shaw pulled his shirt up. "See how I've got these hairs here? Well, as someone who has experienced twink death — Auggie will understand —

Auggie gave a nervous laugh and looked at, of all people, Theo. "Um, I mean, I'm not a hundred percent sure I've gone through twink death."

"That's all right," Shaw told him. "Denial is part of the grieving process."

"Uh —" Auggie made that weird not-laugh noise again. "A little help, Theo?"

Theo lost points because it sounded a little too much like a question when he said, "I was reading my book?"

But the betrayal on Auggie's face made up for it.

"Anyway," Shaw continued, "I've decided that I'm now an otter because — wait, Jem, see this hair right here, the one growing out of my nipple —"

"Are you fucking kidding me?" North shouted. "Put your shirt down. Knock it off. Leave everyone alone. You're not an otter. You're definitely not a muscle otter. And if it's not too much to ask, I'd like to drink my beer and watch thirty fucking minutes of *Pardon the Interruption* without being —"

"Interrupted?" Emery said drily from the kitchen.

North swallowed a scream.

"I can help you," Tean said.

John-Henry choked again. Theo cleared his throat.

"Are you for real?" North said.

"Actually—" Tean began.

"What, like Jem is going to do it? And you'll supervise?"

A hint of color came into Tean's cheeks, and he turned toward Shaw. "I don't know anything about being a muscle otter—"

"Big surprise," North muttered.

"—but I do strength training a couple of times a week. It's an important part of staying healthy, and I could show you with the weights in the basement."

"Finally," Shaw said, directing the words at North, "someone who supports my dream."

"I never said I supported—"

But Tean didn't get a chance to finish because Shaw grabbed his hand and tugged him toward the basement.

Jem was staring at North.

North lasted half a minute before he snapped, "Take a picture. It'll last longer."

"Ok," Auggie said, reaching for his phone.

"Try it, booster seat. See what happens."

Auggie grinned. Jem raised his Goosebumps book to hide his face.

"And you two motherfuckers knock it off in there," North shouted toward the kitchen.

John-Henry called back, "We're literally not doing anything."

"Well, knock it the fuck off!"

Pardon the Interruption came on, but the words ran through North's head, and he couldn't have said what they were talking about or today's specific reason for why Tony Kornheiser needed to be punched in the face. From the basement came the clink of weights, interspersed with Tean's voice, too quiet for North to make out the words.

Then weights crashed, and Shaw screamed.

Theo sat up, worry scribbled across his face.

"I knew it," North said, throwing down the remote. "I fucking knew it!" As he made his way down to the basement, he bellowed, "What kind of fuckery—"

"North!" Shaw was flushed. A tendril of coppery hair clung to his neck. "I did a barbell squat!" He pointed to the barbell, which lay on the floor next to him. "Tean said not to drop it next time."

"And the most important part?" Tean murmured.

"Oh, and the most important part is not to drop it on Tean."

North tried to find words for that. Finally, he settled for a scowl and said, "I thought you got hurt."

"We're fine," Tean said mildly. "Shaw, help me rack the bar on the weight bench."

And because Shaw was Shaw, he did everything exactly the way Tean told him to do it. There was no goofing around. There was no bullshittery. If it had been North, Shaw would have been finding every way from Sunday to rile him up, but instead, he was a perfect fucking lamb.

"No, no, no," Tean said, when Shaw lay back on the bench and grabbed the barbell. "Wait until I tell you."

"Sorry."

"You have got to be fucking joking," North muttered.

When Tean gave Shaw the go-ahead, Shaw grasped the bar again.

"No, no, no." North stomped down the rest of the stairs. "Your hands are too close together."

"North!"

"They need to be wider."

"Leave us alone! Tean is helping me!"

"He does have a point," Tean said. "North, could you show him where?"

With a glare for Tean—it wasn't strictly necessary, but North didn't want the vet getting any ideas—he crossed to the weight bench and shifted Shaw's hands along the steel.

"And when you lift," Tean added, "try arching your back a bit more. You want to feel your chest engage."

North frowned. He'd never heard that before.

Shaw did a set. He was beaming when he sat up. "I did it all by myself. I told you I could be a muscle otter."

"Nobody said you couldn't be a muscle otter," North snapped. "And what about your arms? You think you can be a muscle otter with biceps like those?"

"We were going to do biceps curls—" Tean began.

"I'll show him."

North grabbed a pair of dumbbells, got into position, and performed the first rep slowly so Shaw could watch. He repeated the move again.

Shaw, traitorous weasel fuck, looked at Tean.

"North's got great form," Tean said.

"See?" North said.

Tean watched him for another moment. "North, obviously you don't need any help, but have you ever tried turning your pinkies up slightly on each rep?" He gently turned one of North's hands. "Like this?"

North tried it. Then, grudgingly, he grunted. The noise seemed to be acknowledgment enough for Tean.

"Hey," Jem asked from the stairs. "You guys want some pointers?"

"I was going to show Auggie how I do a fly," Theo said from behind him.

Emery shouldered past them. "I just explained all of this to Colt. I can show Shaw."

"Fuckos," North shouted, "we're in the middle of something!" Then, turning to Tean, he said, "Show me how to do a bent-over row better. Half the time I just feel like I'm killing my shoulders. And you —" That was for Shaw. "— pay attention so he doesn't have to repeat himself."

4

Shaw was bored.

It wasn't anybody's fault, not really. Emery and John-Henry and Colt all had their normal things to do — Emery was cleaning up in the kitchen, and John-Henry was on the couch, working on some very important chief of police stuff that he wouldn't let Shaw look at, not even when Shaw was a spy who army-crawled up behind the couch and then turned into a snake and slithered up to read over his shoulder, and Colt was practicing being a mini-Emery, which meant he was scowling and punching the tip of a pencil through a sheet of paper. And North deserved downtime like anyone else, which was why Shaw felt it was very important to make time for North's hobbies like bill-paying and bill-reading and bill-collecting.

But he was still bored.

Evie came into the room with her arms full of Fashionista Fillies.

Shaw perked up. "Is that Delilah?"

"Daddy," Evie said as she approached John-Henry.

John-Henry made a small noise, his eyes still tracking something on the screen.

"I know that's Delilah," Shaw said. "I'd recognize that mane anywhere."

North shushed him.

"Daddy," Evie said again, adjusting the bundle of fillies so she could tug on his arm. "Play with me."

"Not now, love," John-Henry murmured, although he didn't seem to have heard her.

"DeeDee?" Evie said as she hauled her toys into the kitchen.

"North, I know that was Delilah because of the mane."

North grunted. It wasn't even a particularly good grunt.

"Delilah's basically a collector's item."

"Really?" Ice-rim eyes came up. "How much is she worth?"

"North!"

North made a face and went back to—Shaw wanted to say it was called a spreadsheet, but that sounded too sexual.

"Not right now, Evie," Emery said from the kitchen. "I've got to finish up in here."

When Evie passed through the living room again, Shaw craned his head to follow her. "And I know that's Francesca. She paints her hooves, you know."

"Co?" Evie said as she made her way over to the teenager.

"Oh my God," Shaw said, "that's not just Francesca. That's veterinary anesthesiologist Francesca. You can't even buy her anymore."

"How can a horse be a veterinary anesthesiologist?" North asked in that voice he used sometimes when he kept turning up the TV.

"How can anyone be anything?" Shaw asked in his loftiest voice. "And how dare you?"

"Co, play with me."

"I can't," Colt said, and his glare for some reason was directed at John-Henry. "I have to do this stupid homework."

"Don't say stupid," Evie told him.

Colt glowered and punched the pencil through the paper again.

"If that's Jinx, I'm going to—" Shaw felt some sort of ethereal disturbance at saying *shit myself* to a child (at least, a child who hadn't entered fourth grade), so he found himself at a sudden loss for words.

"If you like the toys so much," Colt snapped, "you play with her."

"Oh my God, can I?"

"Uh, yeah. Please. Be my guest for, like, the next ten years."

"North, is that ok?"

"Whatever."

"John-Henry?"

"Hm?" John-Henry looked up, glanced around, seemed to catch Colt's nod, and mumbled, "Yes, yeah, that's fine," before going back to work.

Shaw helped Evie set up the fillies in order of prettiness.

"I'm Andromeda," Evie said, picking the filly with the spangled hair. "And my parents are dead."

"Uh," Colt said.

"Excuse me?" John-Henry murmured.

"You can be my little sister."

"Oh my God, yes," Shaw said—it was almost, technically, a squeal. "I am your little sister. I'm Chenile, and I'm a court stenographer. Oh, and I have the hugest crush on this stallion named Flame. He has these giant hooves."

"Now I'm a waitress," Evie said over him. "You have to sit over here and order something."

Shaw obediently scooted over. He didn't understand, when he glanced up, the bemused smile on North's face.

5

By the end of the day, North's skin was itching, and he had to get out of the house. It was a low-grade headache. It was the feeling like he was all wires, and somebody had tuned each one to the snapping point. It was the certainty that if he didn't get a cigarette in the next five minutes, he might commit murder. Particularly if Emery came into the living room one more time and said, "And another thing—" before launching into an argument that North had hoped and prayed and dreamed had finally been over.

The night had the sticky persistence of a Midwest summer, but the air was sweet with the smell of wet grass and the distant chirp of the sprinkler. North liberated the emergency smokes from the GTO, found his lighter, and huddled along the side of the house to light up. The first hit made him close his eyes. After the second, he thought maybe, possibly, he wouldn't have to spend the rest of his life in prison for committing murder.

Tires hummed. An engine rumbled. North recognized the sound of the clunker Colt drove—a big old beast of a Ford. But there was a second engine too, and both vehicles were coming in hot.

Headlights came around the corner and raced down the street, and a moment later, tires squealed as Colt turned too sharply into the driveway.

A second car—a BMW, one of the 750i's, silver—came screaming along behind him and parked at the mouth of the driveway, blocking it. Colt dropped out of the truck, and his face was visible in the wash of yellow light from the cab. North caught a glimpse: the wide eyes, the bad color, his lips parted like he was breathing too fast. Then the door slammed shut, and the light went off.

"Hey," North said, forgetting for a moment that, technically, he didn't smoke. He stepped out from the side of the house. "What's—"

Before he could finish, the driver of the BMW got out. He was visible under the streetlight: on the far side of forty, in a white polo and khaki shorts and douche-nozzle shoes, the kind of pinched, balding look that North guessed he spent a lot of money trying to keep under control. He started screaming as he came up the driveway.

"You fucking piece of shit! You hit my car! You think you can just run away after hitting my car?"

Colt bolted toward the house, but North caught his arm. Colt jerked back, spun, and for a moment, didn't seem to see North—he stared at him, face blank with panic. Then recognition clicked, and he looked like he was about to cry.

North squeezed his arm and pushed Colt behind him as the douche-nozzle came up the driveway.

"Hey, I'm talking to you—" the man screamed, stabbing a finger at Colt.

North plucked the cigarette from between his lips and said, "And I'm talking to you. And you'd better keep your fucking voice down because I'm about six decibels away from shoving your teeth down your throat. What's the problem?"

"What's the problem?" the man screamed.

North shifted his weight. He ashed the cigarette.

The douche-nozzle swallowed. In a more moderate tone, he said, "The problem is your kid hit my car!"

"He's not—" Colt began, the words stiff and trembling.

"Did you hit his car?" North asked.

Colt shook his head. A tear spilled and ran down his cheek. "I never came anywhere near him. I parked behind him at the Piggly Wiggly, and when I came out, he was standing there. He started screaming as soon as I got to the truck. I never even touched his car!"

North had heard of this, claiming damage and trying to scare someone into paying. Hell, he'd done some scaring himself a time or two. And with a kid like Colt, too inexperienced to know how to handle the situation, it probably would have worked like a charm.

So, North went with the tried-and-true solution for this kind of scam: he planted a hand on the man's chest and shoved.

The douche-nozzle fell on his ass and—maybe because the man had an inborn flare for the dramatic, or maybe because North didn't know his own strength (he had been hitting the weights a little more frequently, he thought with a bit of satisfaction)—did a complete backwards somersault. He came up slowly, the movements clumsy. Some of that thinning hair was standing up in back, and the collar on his polo was now officially popped. He opened his mouth. "I'm going to sue—"

It was juvenile. It was beyond juvenile—it was childish. North didn't care; he liked a little childishness. Just a little. He lunged, a total fake-out, and the douche-nozzle backstepped so quickly he fell on his ass again. He scrambled to his feet for a second time, sprinted around the car, and shouted from the safety of the driver's door, "You fucking piece of shit!"

"Fuck off," North said. "Fuck you, you miserable fucking fuck of fucks."

The man dove into the car and tore off, and a moment later, Colt and North stood alone on the driveway. Colt snuffled once and wiped his face.

"Don't let a piece of shit like that get to you," North said.

Colt nodded. His gaze came up slowly, and he fixed on the cigarette.

"Fuck," North said under his breath. He flicked the cigarette toward the street. "You didn't see that."

Colt stared at him, eyes wide.

"I was out here working on the car," North said.

Something like a smile touched the corner of Colt's mouth.

"What was I doing?" North asked.

"You were—you were out here working on your car."

North nodded and clapped him on the shoulder. "Good man."

I Can't Even

This story is set before *The Evening Wolves*.

1

"I'm starting to wonder," Emery Hazard said, "if you're willfully misunderstanding my position."

Jessica Haraguchi said, "Hmm," and went back to stamping date due cards.

The Wahredua Public Library was quiet on a December afternoon. It smelled the way it always had—the way it should—like paper and book glue and the heat churned out by the old furnace. Secular winter decorations festooned the circulation desk: snowflakes that, to judge by their irregular design, had been cut out by children during some sort of craft activity; a sweet-smelling cedar garland; a snowman taped to the window, one stick hand holding a book. Which was improbable, of course. How would he turn the pages without tearing them?

The decorations were Jessica's work, of course. She wasn't even thirty yet, and she wore comfortable, sensible clothing. She had zero gray hairs, didn't wear glasses, and had never, once, in all the months of Emery's surveillance, worn a cardigan. Worst of all, not a single recorded incident of shushing since she'd taken over. More than once, Emery had heard children laughing in the library. Laughing.

"I understand that the library has a late policy," Emery said.

The automatic doors whispered open, and Jessica glanced up to smile at the group entering the library—a mixture of men and women, a motley assortment of clothes, heads together as they whispered enthusiastically. Emery suppressed an eye roll at one woman's dinosaur-print button-up. Perhaps they were volunteers, he reminded himself charitably. Perhaps they were here to do something good in the holiday spirit. Perhaps they were going to weed the children's fiction section. They made their way to one of the public meeting rooms.

"I approve of the library's late policy," Emery said.

"I'm so glad," Jessica said.

"As you'll recall, I've even suggested certain amendments. Provisions, if you will."

At that, Jessica raised her head and fixed him with a look. "For the last time, no."

"I—"

"We're not hiring a library investigator."

"The savings in recovered books—"

"Emery, as it is, I don't have the budget to staff the library properly. I can't hire you to go out and recover a ten-year-old copy of *The Phantom Tollbooth* when I can replace it for six dollars."

"In the first place," Emery said, "it's the principle of the matter. An infraction is an infraction, regardless of the monetary value."

"No, it's not."

Voices swelled as the door to the meeting room opened again. The woman in the dinosaur-print shirt emerged and began taping a sign to the door.

"In the second place, I'll remember this cavalier attitude toward acquisitions the next time you turn down one of my recommended titles."

"And as I told you," Jessica said, "I'm not buying *Arctic Mycology II*, not when it's a hundred and seventy dollars, and not when we don't have *Arctic Mycology I*."

"This is why I insist on seeing a full transcript of your graduate coursework."

"Goodbye, Emery."

"Goodbye." He slid *Busy Byzantines: A History of Grist, Wind, and Other Mills in Constantinople* across the desk. "I'm glad you understand that since I've returned this copy—"

"Six months overdue."

"I had to cross-reference—" He stopped himself. He smiled. "Since I've returned this copy, you are now free to waive that ridiculous fine on my account."

"I'm not waiving the fine," Jessica said. "It's a reshelving fine. When you didn't return that book in a timely fashion, we were forced to order a replacement copy—"

"Bullshit."

Jessica actually grinned at him. "Library policy, Emery."

Emery opened his mouth to respond, but then he noticed the sign that had been taped to the meeting room door. It had been done in washable marker, and it said only SHAWNANIGANS.

Which could have meant anything.

But a part of Emery knew it didn't.

"Come around here and take a look at The Stack," Jessica said. There was no way to miss the capital letters. "*Probing the Proboscis: Secrets, Lies, and the Declassified History of the Prehensile Trunk* came in with the last shipment."

"I will not be placated—"

But Emery stopped as a man's voice carried out of the meeting room.

"I don't care if you like him in this story," the man said. "Edison Blaser is an arrogant jackass."

"Edison is Shay's one true love!" That was a woman's voice. "He's got this hard, crusty exterior, but inside, he's warm and gooey."

"Oh," another woman said, "I love the 'soft for you' trope."

"Wait, is it Edison?" That was a third woman. "I thought it was Emerson."

"And that's another thing," the man snapped. "All the names sound the same."

"Emery?" Jessica said. "Did you want—"

He held up a hand.

"Edison really is sweet," one of the women was saying. "Remember when Shay got bit by that vicious puppy, and Edison scared it off?"

"He's unfeeling," the man said. "He's cold. He said all those horrible things to Shay about Shay's sarong."

"But that was after his tender little heart had been crushed by that mean blond man—Norbert, or whatever his name was. You have to understand where Edison was coming from."

"I really think it was Emerson," the third lady said.

Jessica cocked her head, studying Emery, but he was only aware of it distantly. "We just got the feature-length version of *Getting Railed: Cornelius Vanderbilt, Sexual Dynamo*."

"Uh huh," Emery said.

"I think what Emerson and Shawn have is lovely," the first woman was saying. "And the scenes in the library are hot! Remember when he had him strapped to that rolling ladder—"

"And that's another thing," the man sniped. "I think Emerson or Edison or whatever his name is, I think he's impotent."

It was like a nightmare, Emery thought. There was nowhere he could run. Nowhere to hide. He felt like he'd stepped out of his body and was floating toward the meeting room.

"Emery?" Jessica asked. "Is everything ok?"

He waved away the question, managed to say, "Check those out to me," and kept moving toward the meeting room.

Arrogant.

Unfeeling.

Impotent.

He pushed his way into the room, and everyone turned to stare. The woman in the dinosaur-print button-up sat at the head of the table, and she wore a badge that said CHRISTINE – CHIEF OF SHAWNANIGANS. Seated opposite her was a man who had clearly suffered hours under a blow dryer for hair that looked a little bit like a schooner.

"What do you want?" the man barked at Emery. "We're having a private meeting."

"It's not private," the woman—Christine—said. "Did you want to join us? We're a reader group for a local author. Maybe you've heard of him? His name is—"

Emery held up a hand. There were too many impossibilities. That Shaw's stories could have spread this widely. That he could, under even the loosest of interpretations, be considered a local author. That anyone, anywhere, would dedicate themselves to this crap. It was too much for anyone to grapple with.

And so Emery did what he always did: he retreated to solid ground and focused on facts.

"It's not clear to me whether you simply did not read the stories," Emery said, addressing the schooner-haired man at the end of the table, "or if your mental incompetence is of such a staggering degree that you didn't understand them."

Christine covered her mouth.

An apple-cheeked lady's eyes got huge.

"There are no grounds for claiming that Emerson or Edison or any of them are arrogant. I refer you to *Card Catalog Capers*, when he freely admits his cataloging errors while sharing a post-coital moment under the card catalog cabinet. Likewise, the allegation that Emerson is unfeeling is not born out by the events of these stories. Exhibit A: *Unshelved Attraction*, when he confesses his love for Shawn after Shawn is nearly crushed during the earthquake. And any claim of impotence ignores the cornucopia of scenes involving penetration. For the sake of argument, I'll mention only the self-checkout incident in *Inked Pages* and the indecent use of a scanner stand."

The schooner-haired man was choking in anger.

"And don't forget," Christine said, "in *Bound Periodicals* when he's ramming him on that book truck."

"Yes, thank you," Emery said. He glanced around. "Where are the name tags? And have you already discussed the highly improbable use of the charging station in *Passion in the Stacks*?"

2

Normally, Thanksgiving was one of John-Henry's favorite holidays. A big meal. Lots of friends and family. And then, after a couple of hours of good conversation and good food and good football, everyone went home, and he could nap.

Normally, they didn't have friends in from out of town.

A crash came from downstairs, and then a swell of laughter from, of all people, Auggie.

"That," Emery said, "is why I suggested we do something different this year."

"A told-you-so," John-Henry said. "Thank you."

"It's not a told-you-so. I'm simply telling you—"

John-Henry raised his eyebrows.

Emery scowled.

"Nice save."

"John-Henry?" His father's voice came from the front room.

"I bet Shaw cornered him," Emery said.

"Good God."

In the front room, sure enough, Shaw had bracketed Glennworth Somerset between a pair of wingback chairs, and it looked like he was trying to grab his head with both hands.

"If you'd just open your mouth—John-Henry!"

Glenn glared at his son.

"I was just telling your dad about this article I read. Well, it wasn't so much an article as it was a post on Reddit. And it wasn't really much of a post. I mean, it was only a few lines. But this girl was talking about a man who had evil hair and evil eyes and evil teeth, and then he put his—" Shaw mouthed *balls*. "—on a ping-pong table, and—" He laughed. "Oh my God. I just realized maybe they were ping-pong—" He mouthed *balls* again. "And I was telling your dad about it, and he was super interested, and then he ran into a chair, and then I said maybe I should have a look at his teeth, you know, give him a professional opinion—"

"No more Pepsi," John-Henry said, turning him by the shoulders. "Hey, you know what? I heard Evie say she could beat you at the crab walk."

"Oh my God, you know what we should do? We should race!"

"Better go find her."

Shaw sprinted away in a caffeine-infused rush, and John-Henry settled for an apologetic smile and a quick escape from his father.

Another crash came from downstairs, followed by a pained cry and then more laughter. A lot of it.

"I don't want to know," John-Henry said to himself as he started through the kitchen.

He stopped, though, when he saw Cora doing the dishes. "Cora, stop. Don't do that."

Up to her elbows in soapy water, she smiled over her shoulder at him. "Just getting a few things done."

"You already did everything. You don't need to clean up."

"It'll just take a minute."

"Don't do those dishes, please."

He would have pressed the point, but another crash thundered through the house.

"You'd better check on that," Cora said with a tiny smile.

"You're enjoying this."

"You know I always like a good show."

John-Henry had to stop halfway down the steps to stare. The pull-up bar that he'd installed for Colt in the utility room doorway had been ripped from the jambs—no doubt because a pair of jackasses had tried to swing on it at the same time. Those same jackasses were now holding the pull-up bar between them.

"John-Henry, you're up next," Jem said with a grin.

"Ash almost had it last time," Auggie said.

The boy in question was squaring up to the pull-up bar, and Jem and Auggie set themselves. John-Henry didn't realize what was happening until it was too late. All he could do was watch as Ashley grabbed the pull-up bar and swung himself into the air. His target, John-Henry understood in an instant, was Evie's tiny indoor trampoline. And for a moment, it looked like he might make the landing.

Then everything went wrong. Jem and Auggie staggered under Ashley's weight, and their movement sent Ashley off course. Instead of landing on the trampoline, he did a half flip and landed flat on his back. The thud echoed through the basement, and John-Henry heard the breath explode out of Ashley's lungs.

"What in the world—" John-Henry began.

But Ashley was already picking himself up, and Jem and Auggie were cackling like they'd lost their minds.

"You're up next, Mr. Lopez," Ashley wheezed.

"Nobody's up next," John-Henry announced. "The game is over. We're done."

"But—" Auggie began.

"John-Henry—" Jem tried.

"Put it away," John-Henry said, "before somebody breaks their back."

The three boys exchanged glowers as John-Henry headed upstairs.

Emery and Theo were arguing about the scansion of a sonnet at the kitchen table, so he sent them to do the dishes instead of Cora. In the dining room, his mother was complaining about the layout of the desserts. Tean was explaining to Evie and Lana how different indigenous tribes used different parts of reindeer. And John-Henry realized that his first nervous breakdown was going to be on Thanksgiving.

He slipped out into the garage. He needed ten minutes. Maybe less. It would be cold and dark and quiet—

Only it was none of those things. The lights were on. A kerosene heater hissed as it pushed back the chill. And the Mustang and the Odyssey were gone, replaced by Colt's ancient F-150. Two pairs of legs stuck out from under the truck. John-Henry recognized the pair of Adidas that had, in a former life, belonged to him. He also recognized the Red Wings.

"Now give it one of these—yep, like that. Ok, keep loosening the plug, and—" Liquid spattered against plastic. "Fuck yeah, buddy. You did it."

John-Henry sat on the step and watched as the two men worked their way out from under the truck.

"I can definitely do that on my own," Colt was saying as he squirmed free of the truck. "I know there's still a lot I need to learn, but I can definitely do that."

North McKinney was grinning when he emerged, and his eyebrows went up when he saw John-Henry, but all he said was "You're a natural."

Colt's face brightened when he saw John-Henry. "J-H, I changed the oil in the truck. By myself. Well, North showed me how, but I did it."

"You did half of it, bozo. You've still got to change the filter, put it back together, and add new oil."

But for whatever reason, that only made Colt grin harder.

Then John-Henry noticed the coat.

It shouldn't have been a big deal. It shouldn't have been anything, really, because things didn't matter, possessions didn't matter. John-Henry knew that. He'd learned it the hard way, learned it on his own, because it wasn't something his parents had taught him. People mattered, not things.

But the coat wasn't just a coat. It was waxed Bedford cord, and it had chambray pockets and a flannel lining. It was from Vermont. And it had been his birthday present.

Colt still hadn't noticed the oil spattering the cord. He was talking quickly, glancing at North with every other word. "North says you don't have to know how to do everything yourself on your car. He says it's more important to know you can learn how to do things, and cars are just one thing you might want to know how to do. Only he said it better than that. He said it a lot smarter. But I think I like cars, I mean, I know I like them, and I like learning how to do things, and North said he can show me how to change the spark plugs."

North must have noticed the oil because something in his face changed—his expression pulling into a grimace, his mouth opening.

John-Henry let out a breath. He brushed some of Colt's bushy hair away from his forehead. Then he said, "Why don't you show me what you did, bubs? I never learned how to change the oil."

"Figures," North said.

Colt was already clambering under the truck, talking a mile a minute. John-Henry shot North the bird and followed his son.

3

"Because, bunny," Aileen Hazard said as she pulled another box toward her, "you never know what kind of treasures might be in here."

Emery stared at Jem.

Jem wasn't smiling. He wasn't doing anything with his eyebrows. He was sitting cross-legged in a Blossom t-shirt, his full attention seemingly fixed on Emery's mother. Which made it all the more annoying that Emery could tell how amused he was by what was unfolding.

"I highly doubt there are any treasures in a box labeled 'Dad's Records - Old.' Did Dad even have a record player?"

"Don't be silly. Your father loved music."

"What? Funeral marches?"

"Muffin, that's a terrible thing to say."

The corner of Jem's mouth twitched.

"Besides," Emery's mother said, a note of triumph filling her voice as she folded back the cardboard flaps on DAD'S RECORDS - OLD. "This one doesn't even have records. It has some of your old toys."

"Holy shit," Jem said, leaning forward. "I mean, shoot. Sorry, Mrs. Hazard. Is that a Skip-It?"

"That's all right, Jeremiah. I've heard it before, believe it or not." Emery's mother took the Skip-It out of the box, held it by the loop, and swung it once in the air. Jem leaned back in time to avoid getting clobbered, and a grin exploded across his face. Aileen frowned at the Skip-It. "I don't have any idea what it is."

"It's only, like, one of the dopest things ever," Jem said.

"Dopest," Emery said.

"Do you want it?" Aileen asked.

"We should sell it."

"No!" Jem scooted toward the Skip-It, one hand outstretched. "Are you crazy? That's an original. It's priceless."

"Priceless is what people say when they mean something will be exorbitantly expensive." Emery took out his phone. "Do you have an eBay account, Mom, or shall I set one up for you?"

Tean's voice floated in from the front room. "No, the worst thing about a tapeworm is, uh, passing it—"

A woman's voice joined in. "—and seeing the pieces still moving! I know, right?"

"One moment," Emery said and headed toward the entry hall.

"So, Mrs. Hazard, could I maybe see that?" Jem asked. "Just for a minute?"

In the front room, Tean lay on the sofa, a tablet propped up on his stomach as he video-chatted with a woman Emery didn't recognize. She had straight, black hair cut in Birkin bangs, and when she sat back, Emery could read the words printed on her t-shirt: DON'T FORGET—YOU'RE STUCK HERE UNTIL YOU DIE.

Wonderful, Emery thought. He has a friend.

Something must have alerted Tean because he glanced over. His caterpillar eyebrows drew together. "Everything ok?"

"What are you doing?"

"Chatting with Alyssa. She works in the parasitic disease lab at the University of Utah."

This seemed like a much more productive use of Emery's time than rummaging through carefully preserved garbage, but before he could take a seat, plastic clattered against the floorboards in the living room, and Jem whooped in triumph. Emery was surprised to find he remembered the sound. It must have been thirty years since he'd played with a Skip-It, and even then, it hadn't held his attention for long. But the sound was unmistakable. He'd gotten it at Christmas. And, if he wasn't mistaken, his father had gotten it for him. Emery turned back to the living room, the conversation with Tean forgotten. His dad had said something about agility. Something about football. Back then, he'd still had hope.

Jem was grinning like a maniac as he hopped and spun the toy around one ankle, and Emery's mom was laughing and clapping, cheering him on every time Jem looked over for approval. That was surprisingly familiar too.

"Emery, holy—um, crap. Did you know your mom has the best stuff ever? Look at this. Go long!"

Before Emery could do more than process the words, Jem had dropped to his knees, the Skip-It now forgotten, and produced a Vortex football. He reared back and launched it at Emery. Emery caught it more out of reflex than anything else, and the memory came back to him in a flash: spring, the smell of the timothy coming in and the freshly unsealed polyurethane of the football, the ball tucked under his arm, his dad shouting as his mom pinned a sheet to the line.

"Now me!" Jem shouted.

The weight of the football felt right in his hands, and he sent it flying toward Jem, who caught it in a flying jump and crashed into the sofa.

Emery's mom was laughing again, saying, "Be careful, be careful. We don't want to break the sofa!"

"We certainly don't," Emery said. He considered Jem, who was still getting himself upright. "We should take it outside."

"But if you're going to sell it—"

"No!" Jem wailed, and Emery thought it was only thirty percent a joke.

He'd forgotten about selling the toys, and for a moment, he tried to recall why that had seemed like the right idea. Finally he said, "If they have some historical significance, perhaps we should keep them."

"We should definitely keep them," Jem said. "And we should have a Skip-It challenge. And we should make football teams, but I get North because I know he'll cheat."

From the front room came Tean saying, "I'm sorry, but you're not going to beat *Naegleria fowleri*. Brain-eating amoeba? That's got to be the winner."

The woman—Alyssa—said, "Oh yeah? What about *Toxoplasma gondii*? Hijacking the brain? Turning fear into sexual arousal?"

Tean laugh-groaned.

The toys were toys. Emery understood that. He waved off Jem's attempt at another pass, hurried toward the front room, and tried to focus. He was a professional. He had a responsibility to learn as much as possible, about as many subjects as possible, particularly when the words *brain-eating amoeba* came into play.

As he stepped into the front room, Tean craned his head and smiled. "Emery, grab a chair. Alyssa said a bunch of parasites were stolen from the lab, and now they've got a murder pool going."

Bursting out laughing, Alyssa shook her head. "Tean, you can't tell people that!"

"Emery understands."

From the living room came Jem's soft noise of awe, and then Emery's mom saying, "Oh, that was bunny's favorite."

Tean had turned his attention back to the screen, but now it came back to Emery. "Don't you want to sit down?"

"Actually," Emery said, "I think I won't. Maybe you could catch me up on the details later?"

Tean said something, but Emery didn't really hear him. He was already walking back to the living room. And he knew, before he stepped through the opening, what he would see. He'd forgotten, of course. Hadn't thought about it in years. The tiny plastic box that got ridiculously hot—and was completely unsafe for children. The smell of the electric hot plate warming up, and then the slight sweetness of the liquid PVC as it cured. Hadn't thought about all the possibilities of the metal dies. All the hours he'd spent playing with the stupid kit when his dad wanted him to be out catching a football. Or working on his fucking agility.

Jem was playing with the tray on the Thingmaker II, head bowed, his body so tight he was practically quivering with excitement. Emery's mom was smiling, looking a little dazed as she took in Jem's enthusiasm, but her expression changed as her eyes came to rest on Emery. "Is everything all right?"

"Of course," Emery said, kneeling next to Jem to pick up one of the metal dies. Jem was still digging through the box. "It would be impractical to sell all of this. I don't have the time to create the listings, and on an auction site, you're never guaranteed you'll get the value of the items you list."

"It's not really the money, bun—"

"And we have to consider the importance of material culture."

Jem sat up, head cocked, eyes bright.

"We should, of course, test them," Emery said.

Jem's nod came so fast he probably gave himself whiplash. Then his face fell. "There's no goop."

Emery snorted. "You can buy an equivalent liquid PVC at any serious bait-and-tackle shop." He motioned for Jem to take the Thingmaker II as he collected the dies. "The real challenge is going to be creating a die for an accurate scale model of a tapeworm."

4

He was a white man with a fleshy face and a wattle of skin that looked red and scaly, as though maybe he had a rash. His thinning white hair was combed neatly into place. The black three-piece suit made him look like a funeral director, only funeral directors didn't usually spend three or four grand on a suit. His name was Arthur Strickland, and for the next forty-five minutes, all John-Henry had to do was not give him what he wanted.

"Thank you for taking the time to talk to me," John-Henry said. He offered his hand as Strickland stepped into the entry hall, but Strickland ignored it. No, that was too innocent; Strickland saw his hand and pulled back, turtling his arms as though John-Henry might grab him and, in the process, communicate some terrible disease like homosexuality. "I know it took a minute to work out the logistics, but we've got a full house right now, and I wanted us to be able to talk without interruptions."

Strickland made a dry clicking noise in his throat. His watery eyes roamed past John-Henry, taking in the house. John-Henry had seen that look before, usually on B&E guys who were trying to figure out how they'd get in when they came back later.

"Let's sit down," he said as he led Strickland into the front room. "Can I get you something to drink?"

"Water," Strickland said.

"Be right back."

In the kitchen, Emery was chopping potatoes. Furiously.

"I know," John-Henry said.

The chopping got faster. And harder.

Taking a bottle of water out of the fridge, John-Henry said, "It's an hour. Less. He's already crawling out of his skin at the thought of being around real, live queers."

"What a relief that you can joke about letting this bigoted asshole into our home."

John-Henry counted to ten. Then he said, "Ree."

The wire between Emery's shoulders softened. The chopping slowed. "I understand. Your father asked. The asshole has an influential blog." He shook his head again, but it was different this time. "Influential with a bunch of homophobic goat-fuckers."

"An hour," John-Henry whispered, scratching Emery's back lightly through the tee. "Less."

Emery nodded, and John-Henry slipped out of the kitchen.

He had to count to ten again when he handed Strickland the water, though, because Strickland immediately produced a handkerchief—visibly embroidered with a golden cross—and wiped the bottle down. Which suggested, John-Henry thought in a voice that sounded a lot like Emery, that Strickland knew nothing about either homosexuality or contagious diseases. Or basic germ theory. And that last addendum made John-Henry decide, once again, he was going to join an intramural team, get out of the house more, get a subscription to some service that only played Michael Bay movies.

"My father said you wanted to do a profile piece for your blog," John-Henry said.

Strickland made that little clicking noise again. "This is where you live with your homosexual lover?"

This time, he counted backwards from ten. "My husband. Yes."

"And the teenage boy. When did he become part of your relationship?"

From the kitchen came the sound of chopping, the whir of a fan.

"You're talking about our foster son."

Strickland sneered, but only with his eyes. "Yes, I believe that's what you call him."

Breathe in. Breathe out. "Mr. Strickland, we got off on the wrong foot somehow. Why don't we start over? Welcome to our home. I'm grateful you could take the time to talk to me. I'd love for you to meet my family, and I think you'll see that we're happy and loving and—"

Voices rose sharply in the kitchen. "Because I told you to take your shoes off when you come inside!" Emery shouted.

Colt shouted back, "I'm just grabbing my phone!"

"I don't care what you're grabbing. Take your goddamn shoes off!"

Steps hammered away as Colt shot back, "Jesus Christ!"

"Get your ass back here!"

A wordless scream of frustration answered.

John-Henry tried, failed, and rubbed that spot on his forehead.

"How many sexual partners do you have in a week?" Strickland asked.

"In a week?"

That look in his eyes was back. "In a day, then."

John-Henry opened his mouth. He didn't know what he was going to say, but *Get the hell out* sounded about right. Before he could, though, the front door flew open, and North and Shaw tumbled into the room.

"I'm not saying I want to be double- or triple-penetrated," Shaw was saying. He appeared in the opening to the front room a moment later, wearing what John-Henry could only conceptualize as a giant black spiderweb that left ninety-nine percent of his body bare, and a medieval-style codpiece with the face of a devil painted on it. "I'm saying between the two of us, I'd be better at it."

"You'd be better at getting stuffed full of schlong," North said. "Got it."

"You don't have to be snippy about it. It's not your fault. You don't need to feel bad that your sphincter is like a walnut, but like, an old walnut that has been compressed and hardened by time and the seasons—oh, hi! I'm Shaw!"

Strickland was staring. At the codpiece, in particular.

"Who's this bozo?" North asked. And then, voice hardening, "See something you like?"

Strickland flushed, made a choked noise, and started heaving himself out of the chair.

"Mr. Strickland—" John-Henry tried.

But Strickland barreled past North and Shaw—with one last, longing look for the codpiece—and disappeared out the front door.

"He seems nice," Shaw said.

John-Henry sprinted after Strickland, but he hadn't needed to; Strickland had stopped on the porch and was staring at the scene playing out in the yard. Auggie was recording a video on his phone, while Ashley and Colt, dressed in jeans and boots and nothing else, hooked jugs that were—John-Henry prayed—only supposed to look like moonshine and pretended to drink from them—in the process, spilling a lot down their bare chests.

Strickland moaned quietly and licked his lips.

"Ok, but you have to get the jug up as soon as you land after the jump—" Auggie cut off when he saw them. His face filled with color.

"J-H," Colt said, "it's called the Yeehaw Challenge. Have you heard Lil Nas X's 'Old Town Road'? It's so freaking fire."

"You should do it with us," Ashley said with a grin, pushing his hair behind his ears.

"It's a TikTok thing," Auggie mumbled. "They just asked me to record—"

Strickland had recovered himself by then, and his watery eyes slid to John-Henry with a mixture of contempt and expectancy.

For one final moment, John-Henry asked himself how he could still salvage things. Then he looked at his son, the excitement shining through his face, the question there. Because any other day, with anyone else, John-Henry would have already been down there. With his son. Today, though, with this bozo—

Maybe he'd been spending a little too much time with North as well.

Fuck it, he thought. Everything in his body began to unwind, and he took the porch steps down to the lawn. He appraised Colt and Ashley, gave Auggie a wry look that made Auggie grin and blush harder, and said, "I bet if we use safety pins, I could wear that Western shirt your dad has. And we've definitely got to find that hat he wore for Halloween. And ditch the shine jugs, boys. That's a definite no."

Colt traded a rueful look with Ashley and darted inside, and a moment later, Emery started yelling again.

5

"Come on, girl," Colt said in a syrupy voice. He had wedged himself between the sofa and the coffee table, and to judge by the smell of processed lunch meat that wafted up to Emery as he tried to read, he still hadn't given up. "Biscuit, come on. Come here, girl. Come here."

Emery turned a page. Beneath him, a slight scuffing noise came, and then the dog pressed herself even more firmly against his legs.

"Get," Emery ordered.

As usual, the dog ignored him.

"This is so stupid," Colt said, sitting up. A piece of ham dangled from his hand. "Why does she love you? You don't even like her."

"She doesn't love me," Emery said. "She barks at me. Constantly. The other day, when we were having a disagreement about your driving —"

"A disagreement," John murmured from where he lay on the floor.

"Something to add, John?"

He was too good looking, ridiculously so, and the lazy, darting smile still hooked Emery in the gut. It simply wasn't fair. So, instead, Emery turned his attention back to his son. "—she tried to take me out at the ankle because she thought I was attacking you."

"She hates me," Colt said.

"She doesn't hate you. She just doesn't want to sleep with you."

"It's not fair."

John was reading a magazine, pushing fingers through his hair, the swell of one bronzed biceps on display. "No," Emery managed to say. "Most things aren't."

Biscuit chose that moment to dart out from under the protection of Emery's legs and snatch the ham dangling from Colt's fingers.

"God damn it!"

"See?" Emery said. "She likes you."

Colt retreated upstairs, grumbling. The sound of running water and moody teenage stomps suggested he was, finally, getting ready for bed. John lay on the floor, head pillowed on his arm now, leafing through the magazine. Some of the mussed blond hair spilled over his forehead. The lamplight filled the crow's feet around his eyes with shadows. His chest rose and fell smoothly, and where the tee hung askew, dark ink curled across the hard planes of his chest.

"Ree," John-Henry said without looking up.

Emery spread his legs.

"We've got a grown son who's still awake," John murmured as he paged lazily at the magazine. His erection traced a line against the sweat shorts.

"Not for long."

That made him laugh for some reason. He got to his feet. Met Emery's eyes. Touched himself—not much, a brush of his hand that, another time, could have been an accident, or nothing more than adjusting himself. The shorts had slid to expose an inch of the paler skin along his hip, suggesting the curve of his ass.

"You're trouble," he said in that low, throaty way that was barely speech at all.

"Look who's talking."

John stood there another moment, hipshot, light falling along the razor edge of his jaw. Then he said, "I think I'm going to head to bed."

"Uh huh."

"Goodnight, love."

Emery let him go a few feet before he said, "John?"

A soft noise was his only answer.

"Take the blanket."

Laughing again, John draped the blanket over one shoulder to cover himself.

Emery waited until the water in the bathroom stopped and the drama of footfalls ended. Then he made his way upstairs.

"No," Colt was saying. "No! Hold still!"

Emery rapped lightly at the door, and it inched open.

Colt was sitting up in bed, wrangling the puppy against him as he tried to take a selfie. Biscuit squirmed and wriggled and writhed, panting in her desperation to get free.

"Fine," Colt said, releasing her. "Get out of here!"

Biscuit bounded to the foot of the bed, gazed up at Emery, and yapped once.

"She's defective. You got me a broken dog."

"The risks you take when you rescue a mutt trapped inside a garbage can." Emery scooped up Biscuit, pressed his head to hers, and whispered, "Keep it up. Evie wants to be Cruella de Vil for Halloween."

Biscuit yapped again—this time, directly in Emery's ear—and licked his face.

He set the dog down, scooted her in Colt's direction, and said, "Stay."

Whining, Biscuit turned in a circle once.

Emery stared.

Biscuit slunk over to Colt, tail drooping.

"I changed my mind," Colt said, but then he gave the words the lie by ruffling her ears. "I don't want you."

It didn't seem to bother Biscuit much; a moment later, she and Colt were tangled together, and the dog was already snoring.

"I don't want her sleeping with you."

"I know."

"Put her in her crate before you go to bed."

"I said I know."

When Emery let himself out of the room, he could hear Colt whispering, "Bro, look at this," and Ashley's answering note of adorableness.

In the bedroom, the light spilled over everything like silk. Like samite, Emery thought. Over the familiar lines of his husband: his bare foot, a long, lean leg, the hollow of his thigh, rising and falling with his chest.

"Took you long enough," John said.

Emery bumped the door shut with his hip and tugged off his shirt. "Just making sure we weren't interrupted."

Good Vibes Only

This story is set after *The Evening Wolves*.

1

"I thought this was a date night," Auggie said in a low voice. "I thought you were taking me on a date."

"I am taking you on a date, Auggie. I'm taking you to a movie that you want to see. I know you want to see it because you've said on three different occasions—loudly—something to the effect of 'Boy, I'd sure love to see *Wonder Woman 1984*.'"

"Ok, you get points for paying attention."

"You printed out the movie times."

"Now you're losing points."

"You did a huge stretch in bed this morning and said, 'Gee, I wonder if we should go on a date tonight and see a movie.'"

"Zero points, Theo. You're right back where you started. And you still haven't explained why you invited Orlando."

Ahead of them, Orlando was pressed up against the snow-dusted bricks of the movie theater, attempting to suck his girlfriend's face off. Nat was giving as good as she got. Drake, their boyfriend, was scrolling on his phone.

It was one of those perfect winter nights that came between Christmas and New Year's, when kids are out of school and adults find ways to take extra days off work, and in good years, the snow stayed white and powdery, instead of hardening into black-crusted slags. Jefferson Street was busy with pedestrian traffic. A pack of teenage boys trampled past Theo and Auggie, their attention locked on a group of girls who were trying to take selfies in front of a snowman. An elderly woman in a snazzy suit power-walked right through the pack, taking the boys out like they were bowling pins. From the other direction, a trio of Wroxall college kids—ones who hadn't gone home over break—smoked and worked way too hard to look cool in beanies.

"Stop looking at their beanies," Theo murmured.

"It's not fair," Auggie said. "It's such a good look, and my head is totally the wrong shape."

"Your head is the perfect shape. I love your head."

"One point. This date is finally starting to head in the right direction." The line lurched forward, and Auggie snapped, "Orlando, Nat, break it up before I have to call the fire department."

Orlando managed to separate from his girlfriend after a final, soul-sucking kiss. He blinked owlishly at Auggie and then said in a tone of utter delight, "Augs! When did you get here?"

"Let it go," Theo whispered.

"Sorry," Drake said with an apologetic smile as he chivvied the lovebirds toward the ticket booth. "Nat's been traveling a ton, and I've been way too busy at work, and Orlando's feeling neglected."

"You don't need to apologize," Theo said.

"Let's not be too hasty," Auggie said, but he waited until Drake and Nat and Orlando were far enough ahead that they couldn't hear him. He added, "And you still haven't explained why Orlando is here."

"I thought you invited him," Theo said.

"I did not."

"Huh. Maybe it's like how he ended up having the bedroom next to yours in the Sigma Sigma house. Maybe you guys have a psychic connection."

"We'd better not. He tried to tell me about his sex life with those two. I'm telling you, Theo, my sweet, tender, innocent mind. If we have a psychic connection, I'm going to turn into a sex fiend."

"Nobody's been a sex fiend since the '80s," Theo said as he nudged him forward.

They bought their tickets and made their way into the lobby of the historic theater. The Bijou was one of those wonders of preservation, with most of the original design and décor still in excellent condition: the red-and-gold-and-cream color palette of the lobby, the plaster chevrons patterned across the ceiling, even the decorative panels worked with Art Deco geometry.

Auggie inhaled deeply and said, "Popcorn."

"I'll get it," Theo said.

"No," Auggie said. "I got it. Go grab us seats so we don't end up sitting in the front."

He got popcorn. He got two Cokes. He lost track of the throuple in the chaos, which was fine by him. He was aware of a faint static buzz building at the back of his head.

When he got into the theater, every seat was filled. Theo sat in the front row, waving for Auggie. Orlando sat right next to him.

"You've got to be kidding me," Auggie said.

"Sorry."

Auggie passed him the Cokes and turned himself out of his coat and scarf. He had barely dropped into his seat before the lights went down. Theo was twisted around in his seat, looking toward the back of the theater.

"Theo," Auggie whispered. "The movie's starting.

"I know," Theo said, "but I swear to God, I thought I saw Jem —"

Then the projector began to run, and light painted the screen. Theo turned back around. A moment of pure and total panic seized Auggie.

And then Fer's face appeared on the screen. He leaned back, looked straight into the camera, and then turned his head to speak to someone out of the frame. In this case, it had been Auggie. And this had been the best take out of approximately a hundred.

"I know it's running, Augustus. I don't care. He needs to hear it from me, so you'd better put it right at the beginning of your fancy-lad movie."

Theo's breathing sounded funny. He looked at Auggie, his eyes huge, his mouth moving like he thought he was supposed to laugh.

Faintly, Auggie heard himself say, "Ok, Fer, Jesus."

Fer scratched his nose with his middle finger. His attention came back to the camera. When he began to speak again, Theo's head swiveled back to the screen as though it had been pulled.

"Listen up, dipshit: if you hurt him, I'm going to kill you. There. My last brotherly duty is done, thank fucking God. Boner, how do you turn this camera off?" Fer reached for the camera, and something beeped, but the recording continued. Standing, Fer rubbed a hand between his legs and said, "This crotch rot is eating me the fuck alive."

Orlando started giggling uncontrollably.

"What—" Theo began.

But the movie cut to the next clip: it was from one of their summer float trips, Auggie adrift in a canoe and trying to shield himself as Theo splashed him with water. The sun turned the river into a mirror, and Auggie could hear the mixture of delight and outrage in his shrieks. Then he lost his paddle, and the current turned him, and Theo started laughing so hard that he couldn't splash anymore, and the camera began to wobble.

The next clip was Lana's first birthday party back home. Orlando had filmed this one, and now the dumbass made a soft noise like he had zero memory of it and like this was the cutest thing he'd ever seen. Theo and Auggie sat on either side of Lana, helping her blow out the candles on her cake. Theo tucked Lana's dark hair behind her ear without seeming to think about it. The Auggie on the screen looked so much younger, and he was so excited to help her blow out the candles that he didn't notice. But the Auggie in the theater noticed, and he thought, You cannot cry, you cannot cry, you cannot cry.

Again the image changed: moving day, the boxes lining the hallway of their new home, Auggie trying to document everything with his phone. He found Theo on the floor in the empty living room. Theo's t-shirt was sweat-dark and pasted to his chest. Because of how he lay, with his feet planted and his knees higher than his body, his shorts had slid down to expose most of his legs. In the video, Theo still hadn't noticed Auggie; he was scrolling on his phone. And then he dropped the phone, smiled up at Auggie, and said, "Welcome home, babe."

Clip after clip. The night they'd gone "camping" in a blanket fort Auggie and Lana had built together. Theo had surprised them with a star projector he'd borrowed from the library, and they'd toasted marshmallows over a tiny propane flame. Theo asleep on the deck, startling awake when Auggie and Lana got him with water guns, his beer falling right into his lap. The first time Lana had seen the ocean, on their trip to Gulf Shores, and the wonder that had made her small face luminous. Theo in bed, reading a book, one arm behind his head. And then he noticed the camera and set the book aside, laugh lines deepening as he said to Auggie, "Come here."

The final shot was a close-up of Auggie's face. Just his eyes, really. Crinkled with happiness. And Auggie whispering, "I love you." He didn't remember taking the video, but he'd found it in their shared cloud backup because Theo had kept it.

The projector turned off. In the dimness of the house lights, Auggie got on one knee. He palmed the ring from Orlando. And only then did he risk looking up at Theo.

He was crying, of course. Tear tracks looked like star trails on his cheeks. But he was smiling too.

"Daniel Theophilus Stratford," Auggie said, it didn't matter that he'd rehearsed this a hundred times, or that he'd spent his life acting and pretending and learning each part by heart, or that he loved Theo, and that in a way, it shouldn't have felt like a risk because, after all, Theo had already asked him. In this moment, his heart hammered so loudly he could barely hear himself speak, and his voice was thready and rough by turns. "When I met you, I didn't know what I wanted out of life. I didn't know who I wanted to be. But I did know, the minute I saw you, that I wanted you."

Laughter rippled through the audience.

That eased something in Auggie's chest, and he took a deep breath and smiled, and Theo reached down to run his fingers along the side of Auggie's face.

"Everything I am today is because of you. I'm a better person because of you. I'm happy because of you. Every day I get to spend with you is this amazing, wonderful gift that I never expected to have. And I want to spend the rest of my life with you. Will you marry me?"

Theo's fingers grazed his cheekbone, and he whispered, "Yes."

Orlando shot to his feet. "He said yes!"

Cheers erupted as their friends and family moved down to congratulate them, and Auggie turned his head up for a kiss.

2

"This is impossible," Tean said.

Jem put his hands on his hips. "I mean, it's not not impossible."

Tean didn't know what that meant. He couldn't bring himself to ask.

The Stratfords' barn was, to put it frankly, a disaster. It was old, but that wasn't necessarily a problem. The seasoned hand-hewn beams were actually lovely, and the outside was charmingly rustic. It had never been used for livestock, so it smelled mostly like hay and the cold concrete slab, and those were all smells that could be easily taken care of. But it was, unmistakably, a barn. And thanks to Jem's overexcited offer to help, Tean now had twenty-four hours to turn this into the perfect reception hall for Theo and Auggie's wedding.

"I can't believe this is the first place they pounded pork," Jem said.

That penetrated Tean's fog. He turned to look at his husband and asked, "What?"

"I mean, a barn? Ok, ok. I guess I can see it. Theo's out here, doing his thing, looking all ripped and tough, and maybe he throws a bale of hay like it's nothing, and Auggie just spasms because he knows Theo could do that to him, and he's thinking about Theo's eyes, which are the absolute perfect blue—" Jem seemed to hear himself. He offered a slightly too charming smile, held up a finger, and said, "What were you saying?"

"I wasn't saying anything. You, on the other hand, were describing your ideal man."

"No! No, no. I was simply explaining, under the circumstances, how an impressionable young boy like Auggie—you know, I can see why this is where he let Theo butter his biscuit for the first time."

"What?"

"The devil's dance. Smashing slinkies." Jem peered into Tean's face. "Sex?"

"I know what you're talking about! I don't know why you're talking about it here!"

"Because that's why we're having the reception here."

Tean counted to ten in his head. Then he said, "No. It's not."

"It's not?" Jem appraised the barn again. "Then why are we having their reception in an old barn?"

"Because," Tean said. He felt like he might be choking on something. "It's the only way Theo's family will have anything to do with the wedding. They won't attend the ceremony. So, we're having the reception here."

"Ok, but then, why aren't they helping?"

Tean held himself very still. And then he said, "Jeremiah."

"You know what?" Jem said in an oh-so-bright voice. "I'm going to get the fairy lights."

For the first hour, all they did was clean. Fortunately, the barn was already empty, so it was mostly a process of Tean sweeping and getting down the cobwebs and pretending not to hear when Jem said things like "Tean, look at this," and "Tean, what do you think this is?" and Jem pretending an old pitchfork was his penis, and Jem saying, "Ok, but seriously, I think I'm caught in these lights."

Tean chose to operate under the belief that Jem would either free himself or die trying. He was prepared to accept either outcome.

Once the barn was clean and, against all odds, the fairy lights were strung, Tean began setting up the folding tables and chairs while Jem hung the drapery—long, white sheets that softened the barn's bare wood—and added greenery. Yes, the greenery was plastic. Yes, it was terrible for the environment. Yes, the use of fake greenery in a real barn in the middle of winter was a grotesque example of capitalism —

"I can hear you all the way up here," Jem said from the ladder.

Tean scowled at him.

"Whoa, whoa, whoa," Jem said and pretended to wobble. He grinned and waved his free hand. "I'm fine." Then the ladder rocked under him, and he screamed and wrapped his arms around a post. "Oh shit!"

Moments passed. Jem, it appeared, would not be falling to his death.

Tean started putting on the chair covers.

"I'm fine, by the way," Jem announced.

He was finishing the chairs when Jem's excited "Oh my God, Tean, come here!" made him shudder.

But, because he was a glutton for punishment, he made his way toward the sound of Jem's voice. He stopped at the barn door. And he stared.

Goose and Peppermint, the Stratfords' old dogs, were playing tug-of-war with one of the table runners, while Jem recorded them on his phone. "Babe," Jem said, "this is seriously the cutest thing ever. Look how much fun they're having! Oh, we should teach Scipio to—"

Tean waded into the fray. He pried the tablecloth from Goose's jaws, and then he turned on Peppermint. The dog wagged her tail, but when Tean said, "No," she dropped her end of the runner.

"Jem," Tean said.

"Sorry, sorry, sorry. I was going to take it away from them, I swear."

"This is very stressful for me."

"I know."

"We've got a lot to do."

"I know. I was just—"

"Please help me."

Jem's smile faded. "Yeah, babe. Ok. I'm really sorry."

Tean carried the runner into the barn and set it aside. He was pretty sure that Emery and John-Henry had a steamer he could use to fix it.

After that, the work progressed steadily—although there were, still, a few setbacks. In the process of building the photobooth, which was mostly a matter of an Allen wrench and lot of IKEA-style parts, Jem managed to get himself trapped inside. That meant Tean had to remove the door, which meant temporarily abandoning the party favors, which meant when he finally rescued his husband, Goose and Peppermint were nosing through the scraps of ribbon and custom bookmarks.

"I followed the instructions," Jem said. "I swear to God."

He was still wearing one of the wax mustaches, which wasn't helping his case.

The final straw came when—as Tean began setting up the centerpieces—he caught Jem building a house of cards out of the bookmarks.

"You know what?" Jem said as he scrambled to his feet. "I'm going to finish the centerpieces for you. I'm going to do it right now."

But he looked so miserable that Tean's anger washed out of him. Jem was good at so many things. On another day, if Tean hadn't been so stressed and hadn't gotten caught up in his own anxiety about the project, he would have realized the way to enlist Jem's help would have been to make a game of it, or to take more time to explain how he needed help so that Jem could do what he always did—make Tean's life better.

"I'm sorry I haven't been patient today," Tean said. "I'm feeling overwhelmed, and I shouldn't be taking it out on you. You've been trying all day to make this fun. That's what I should have been doing too. This is for our friends, and we love them, and we should be happy about the opportunity to show them how much we love them."

Jem's smile was reluctant. "I'm sorry I wasn't a good helper."

"You've been a very good helper. You did so many things for me, and I really appreciate it. The house of cards idea is really cute—do you think there's a way we could incorporate that into the table decorations?"

His smile grew. "Actually, I was thinking—"

Tean's phone buzzed, and he recognized the number of one of the party supply stores he'd contacted. He answered.

"Where do I leave the balloon arch?" a man asked.

Tean moved to the barn doors. The only car he could see was their rental. "Sorry, where are you? Maybe you've got the wrong address?"

The man rattled off the Stratfords' address. And then he said, "You going to pick this up or what?"

"What do you mean? I paid for the delivery."

"Yeah. I'm here. I'm delivering it."

"And I'm telling you, you're not here. I'm here. I think I would know."

"Buddy, I'm parked on the state fucking highway. You want this balloon arch, you can come out here and get it. I'm not ruining my suspension driving down to that fucking barn." The man took a breath. "Now, do you want it or not?"

Tean opened his mouth, but Jem took the phone from him and said, "I'll be right there."

"No," Tean said, "that's not fair. I paid—"

A grin slanted across Jem's face. "I got this."

3

The doorbell rang, and Shaw steadied his penis hat.

"I'll get it," Auggie said. His own penis hat wobbled as he stood up suspiciously fast.

"No, no, no! It's your party. You have to be the first one to get a pacifier."

One of the hardest parts of being in charge of a bachelor(ette) party, Shaw decided, was that so many people simply didn't know the etiquette. Auggie hadn't known he was supposed to hump the six-foot-tall inflatable pink penis while they shouted encouragement. And he hadn't even known a penis veil existed, let alone that he was supposed to wear one. He had seemed excited about the penis straws, but that might have been because he kept saying he needed a drink.

"I'll get it," North said, clomping in his giant boots toward the front door. As he left, he added, "You've probably heard this before, Strawberry Shortcake, but the quicker you get on your knees and use your mouth, the quicker this will be over."

Another of the hardest parts of being in charge of a bachelor(ette) party was North.

Auggie gave a long look at the plastic tub, which Shaw had filled halfway with water and then liberally strewn with pacifiers. He caught the veil as it fell into his face again and said, "Aren't you supposed to do this at baby showers?"

"Isn't a lot of this stuff for baby showers?" Jem asked—unhelpfully in Shaw's opinion.

True, throwing a last-minute bachelor(ette) party had been more difficult than Shaw had expected, but when Auggie and Theo had decided— with six days to spare—to get married on New Year's Eve, Shaw had been willing to rise to the challenge. North, less so. In fact, when Shaw had his third hysterical crying meltdown in the party aisle of the Dollar Tree, North had said something along the lines of "What is the big deal?"

Which, Shaw thought with a little swell of vicious satisfaction, had not gone well for North.

In the end, they'd managed to transform Emery and John-Henry's home into a facsimile of a Grade A bachelor(ette) party. Foil curtains designed to look like hearts and stars and disco balls covered the walls. Heart and rainbow and, yes, penis-shaped balloons floated everywhere Shaw had been able to make them fit. The banner said LET'S GO GIRLS, and both Emery and Tean had remarked on the missing comma.

True, the blue and pink plates (patterned with tiny baby footprints), hadn't come from the bachelor(ette) party collection. And neither had the tablecloth, which showed an exploding confetti popper and the words BABIES BE POPPIN'. The games had been the hardest part—Shaw didn't really know any bachelor(ette) party games, and so he'd gone with the standards: bobbing for pacifiers, baby food taste test, and of course, candy bar in a diaper. When Emery had arrived, bringing Auggie back from dinner, he had taken one look at the diapers laid out on the table, a candy bar neatly presented in each one, and said, "No."

Now, though, the party balanced on a tipping point. It would either be a tremendous success (of course), or it would lose momentum. He scanned the room—Emery, Auggie, Tean, Jem. The first three were still staring into the tub of pacifiers. Jem, though, with his usual perceptiveness, glanced up and met Shaw's eyes. Then he made a face.

"Come on," he said, squeezing Auggie's shoulder. "It's actually way harder than it looks, and it's pretty fun. You do the first round, and then I'll go."

"How did you sterilize the tub?" Emery asked.

Shaw chose to ignore that.

As Auggie got down on his knees, North came back to the living room with John-Henry. "It was just this dud."

John-Henry gave North a look and then said, "I thought I'd better knock in case things were getting wild. I promise I don't mind staying at my parents' tonight if you guys are going to let loose."

"Theo would kill me if we did anything too crazy," Auggie said. "Come get a nipple in your mouth with me."

Laughing, John-Henry undid his tie and joined Auggie next to the tub. "Not to brag, but I killed it at this game when we did this for Evie's baby shower."

"I told you it was a baby shower game," Auggie said.

"That has got to be the lamest flex in the history of the world," North said. "So what? You got a bunch of nipples in your mouth? We already knew you were the town fucking-post before you got all worn out and saggy."

"Saggy?" Tean murmured.

Jem's eyes were bright. "So many questions. How many nipples in your mouth is considered impressive? What is a fucking-post? Please describe at length. Um, which parts of John-Henry are worn out and which parts are saggy?"

"Thank you, Jem," John-Henry said.

"Just play the game!" Shaw said. Firmly.

Perhaps a little too firmly, considering how everyone went silent and looked at him.

A knock at the door seemed to unpause everyone.

"Thank fucking God," North muttered as he headed toward the front door.

"Now," Shaw said, "I'm going to start a timer, and you try to get as many nipples in your mouth—"

A rumbly, sexed-up voice said, "I've only got two, but I can help you get started."

The man wore a pair of navy trousers and a matching shirt that hung open across his chest. A silver badge suggested he was from the "spread 'em" school of law enforcement. He was twentyish, dark haired, with impossibly defined abs, pecs, shoulders, and biceps, all glistening under what Shaw suspected was a mist of baby oil.

"Make that four," another man's voice said. He was around the same age, had the same kind of body, and had dark brown skin. He wore chaps that accentuated bulging thighs and a tiny silver pouch that hid nothing of his dick. Boots with spurs and a tiny vest completed the outfit.

A third said, "Oops, make that six." This one was dirty blond, and he'd gone with a football theme: white shoulder pads dusted with glitter, tight white shorts, a silver mesh cup that left him even more exposed than the cowboy.

"Eight, sweetheart." This one had hair like cornsilk and baby blues, and he'd gone for the fallen angel look: white-and-silver wings, a tiny feathered jock.

Shaw stared at the four men.

Everyone stared at the four men.

"What," Shaw said, "the fuck?"

"More or less what I was thinking," Emery said.

Tean had covered his eyes with one hand, and Jem was trying— between bouts of giggles—to pull his hand down and make him look.

"They're strippers," North said.

"What are they going to strip?" John-Henry asked. "They're pretty much naked already."

"They can dance, then," North snapped. "Auggie, which one do you like the most?"

"Uh." A blush turned Auggie's face to fire. "You know, I don't think—"

"The football one," Jem said.

"No, I—"

"Obviously it's the football one," Emery said.

"There you go," North said, and he gave the football player a shove toward Auggie. "Grind on him for a while until he stops looking so pathetic. The rest of you, pick your poison. Oh, stay away from him." He indicated Emery. "He bites."

Emery bared his teeth in what couldn't be mistaken for a smile.

Shaw could feel the party slipping away from him. For the moment, he set aside the fact that North had done this without asking him, much less without consulting the party vision board that Shaw had worked so hard on. He focused on getting things back under control. "We'll have time for grinding later. Right now, we've got these games—"

"Nobody wants to pretend to eat a baby's dump, Shaw," North said. "Here, you can have the cowboy."

"I don't want the cowboy."

"Why not? He's a stud."

"He's totally a stud," Jem said. He was still fighting to lower Tean's hand. "Just like the fallen angel is the one North is going to bang."

"Nobody's banging anybody," John-Henry said mildly. "Valentino, do I make myself clear?"

The fallen angel ducked his head and mumbled, "Yes, Chief Somerset."

Another long silence passed before Emery said, in a deadly voice, "Interesting."

"Ree, come on. I arrested him."

"I'm sure you did."

"Good Lord."

"Tell you what," Shaw said, "the strippers can help with the talent show—"

"Talent show?" North said. "I'm not paying these guys by the hour so they can be the backstage crew for your one-man production of *Evita*."

"Oh my God," the one in the police uniform said. "I know how to swallow swords."

"You'd goddamn better," North said. "Now somebody put some music on, and somebody else get over and rub your butt on that little wiener over there."

"Ok, um, North?" Auggie got to his feet, and he held out a hand to ward off the football player—while making a visible effort not to look directly at him. "I really appreciate this. It's super cool of you, and so generous, and normally, it would be a ton of fun."

"He didn't ask me," Shaw said. Loudly. "That's why it doesn't go with the theme of the party."

"But," Auggie said before North could speak, "I'm not, uh, comfortable with this."

"Plus Theo would kill him, kill the stripper, and then kill you," Tean said, now holding a pillow in front of his face. "Should I call them strippers? I'm sorry if that was offensive."

The football player cooed, his eyes raking Tean up and down, "Oh Daddy, you are delicious."

Mid-wrestle, Jem seemed to forget about the pillow he was trying to take away from Tean. He sat up straight, his eyes sharpening on the football player.

"It was very nice of you boys to get dressed up and come over here," Shaw said, "but as you can see, we already have a full night planned —"

"Don't be ridiculous," Emery said in that same deadly voice. "John and Valentino haven't seen each other in — how long did you say, John?"

"I honestly cannot believe you right now."

"That long, really?"

"The strippers aren't going anywhere," North said. "I already paid them for three hours."

"Quit looking at him," Jem said to the football player.

The football player was practically purring.

"All right," Auggie said. "Let's all take a break. I think North was right. Let's put on some music. Let's relax. Everybody — everybody — have a drink or eight. And then we'll play Shaw's games. North, these guys can help with the party stuff. Sound good?"

"What a fucking waste," North said.

"I don't want them eating the cocktail wienies," Shaw said.

"Perfect," Auggie said. "Let's do some shots."

Someone put on music. Dua Lipa. Then Lizzo. The cluster in the living room broke up. Auggie lined up shots in the kitchen with Jem and two of the strippers — the cowboy, it turned out, was Spike, and the football player was Maverick. Shaw decided a shot wouldn't hurt his nerves, just the one, so he joined them. One shot turned into two. And two turned into three. And the music was definitely louder. And the party had a swimmy, underwater quality. And his stomach was turning inside out and simultaneously being a bagpipe, and he was starting to remember why he didn't usually drink.

That was why, when he turned around and saw Emery looming over Valentino while the fallen angel frowned at a piece of paper, biting on the eraser of a pencil, he wasn't sure he was hearing them correctly.

"—not just a surgical technician," Emery was saying. "You have a lot of options: solar photovoltaic installer, for example, or massage therapist, or an amusement park ride safety inspector. But you won't know what's best until you complete the career aptitude test."

"My high school counselor had me do one of these after I sucked him off," Valentino said. "It said I should be a riverboat captain."

"Was it the Johnson O'Connor model? Because that's outdated."

"It was definitely a johnson," Valentino said with a smirk.

Emery pointed at the paper. "No more talking; take the test."

A big underwater-slash-bagpipe wave carried Shaw out of the kitchen and into the living room, where John-Henry was leaning against the wall, chatting with the stripper cop—Kalvin, he had told them. With a K.

"Dude, these are the exact same pants the police wear," Kalvin was saying, pointing to his pair of navy trousers. "Let me guess—they ride up all the time, and your underwear starts bunching up."

John-Henry gave him a disbelieving smile. "Ok, I was seriously just complaining about that to Emery the other day."

"That's what I'm telling you. I try to be authentic. What you do, though, is you just take them in a little right here, and they fit like a dream." He turned around and did a little bounce on his toes. "Plus, they make my ass look bangin', right?"

"I'm sold," John-Henry said with a laugh. "Who do you use?"

"Bro, I do it myself. I'll text you my address, and you can drop them off. I'll have them done in a day."

Shaw realized the room was getting a little more vertical than usual. He put out a hand to catch himself and stumbled into Jem. Jem steadied him automatically. His eyes looked a little red, and his voice sounded thicker than usual as he said, "Where the fuck is he?"

Shaw tried to ask, "Who?" but what came out was "Whum?"

"Fucking Maverick. I take my eyes off him for one minute—" He glanced around the room, shouted, "Tean?" and headed into the kitchen.

Without Jem's support, Shaw found himself lurching down the entry hall. The murmur of voices from the front room called him, and he managed to catch himself at the next opening and lean against the wall.

In the front room, Tean stood in a corner, an inflatable penis held in front of him the way sometimes, in movies, people held a cross to keep a vampire at bay. The football player—Maverick—had a hand planted on either side of Tean, penning him in.

"I just want to talk," he was saying. "What's so bad about talking?"

"You know who loves talking?" Tean asked. "Jem. Why don't we find Jem?"

"I get so bored with guys my own age," Maverick said over him. He changed the way he was standing, and suddenly, with that tiny shift, every muscle seemed to pop. "I've always been an old soul, and I want someone I can be serious with. You know what I mean? Like, I'd love to find someone who is really grounded, you know? Plus, sex with older guys is always off the chart. Like, what it does to me, the way it affects my body."

"You!" Jem shouted from the entry hall.

"Whoa, man, whoa!" Maverick backpedaled, hands raised in surrender. "We were just talking!"

"What the fuck is going on in here?" North asked. The cowboy, Spike, drifted along behind him, carrying the bowl of M&Ms. North held out a hand, and Spike dutifully poured M&Ms into his palm.

"Nothing, man!" The eye black Maverick had applied made the panic in his expression even more apparent. "We were just talking!"

"He's hitting on Tean, and not in the this-is-so-awkward-I-can't-get-enough-of-it-way!" Jem shouted over him.

"Someone please make me stop holding this penis," Tean said.

At that moment, the front door opened, and Theo stepped into the house.

Everyone stopped talking. The music continued faintly in the background. Shaw's stomach bagpiped again.

Theo's gaze moved from North to Spike to Jem to Tean to Maverick to Tean again and finally to the plastic penis. His keys jangled as they swung from one finger. Finally, in a neutral voice, he said, "I thought I was supposed to pick up Auggie."

"Dr. Stratford?" Spike said. A smile glowed on his face, and he shoved the bowl of M&Ms at North. "Mav, Val, this guy was the dopest teacher for tenth-grade Language Arts." Squaring himself up with Theo, his smile spreading, he said, "Dr. Stratford, it's going to be an honor to grind your balls off."

4

"There's an entire tradition," Emery was trying to explain to John, "of murders happening at weddings."

John just patted his arm. "I know, love."

Gabby Lopez, the most likely candidate for said murder—in Emery's mind, at least—gave another hiccupping wail and tried to clutch Auggie's hand as she moaned, "My baby's leaving me."

The best word for how Auggie looked was stunning. He'd always been annoyingly attractive, and now, in a dusty rose suit and floral tie, with his hair slightly different (Jem had given the crew cut an update—Emery didn't have the right words for it, but he wanted to say it was…slantier?) and the clean line of his jaw, he was perfect. Even the scar, which Shaw and Cora had attacked with a makeup kit, added to the effect—a thin white line that gave otherwise blandly perfect features character.

To his credit, Auggie handled his mother with surprisingly good grace. He broke her hold with an easy twist of his wrist—Theo must have taught him that one, Emery decided—and moved across the room as he said, "Ok, what about my bag?"

They were in the bridal suite, which (when someone wasn't paying two thousand dollars a pop to use it) doubled as the vestry for Wroxall's Bayne Memorial Chapel. It was an imposing neogothic structure that, in keeping with the times, was also nicely nonsectarian. To the extent, Emery had been surprised to learn, that they even let a couple of homos get married there.

North, of course, hadn't missed the opportunity to make as many jokes as possible about Auggie-the-bride before Tean had sent him to hand out wedding programs to the guests.

"Your bag is packed," John said. "Tean packed it for you." Auggie opened his mouth, and John added, "Jem double-checked it."

"Thank God," Auggie said under his breath.

"He packed you two first aid kits."

"Which I still insist is a reasonable precaution," Emery said. "What if you lose one?"

"Uh huh," John said in the same tone he occasionally used after Emery did a particularly thorough job summarizing a documentary.

"What if you need two tourniquets and each kit only has one?"

"Good point, love."

It was the same tone, Emery was beginning to suspect, he sometimes got when John was deep into a show on ESPN.

"What about the caterers?" Auggie whipped around. "Oh my God, what about the venue?"

"We're already in the venue," Emery said. "This is the venue. If they don't like it, they're going to have a hard time kicking us out."

For some reason, that made John give him a look.

"Also," Emery added, "North and Shaw gave them the final check."

"I'm going to be all alone," Gabby wailed. She threw herself into one of the armchairs, head thrown back, arms flung wide. She was a distinctly attractive woman, and she was making a point not to actually cry—Emery decided he'd start to get worried once she ruined her mascara. "Everyone leaves me."

Auggie got a little too close to her on his next pace, and she grabbed him again. He tried to pry her hand free, but she had a better grip this time—or was a little more determined. "I'm not leaving you, Mom. I love you. And I've been living with Theo for years. Nothing's going to be different."

"It is different." Gabby struggled to sit up—either because she was overcome by emotion or because the old armchair lacked adequate lumbar support. "It is. You're my baby. I poured all my love into you, and I knew one day you'd come back to take care of me so I wouldn't be alone forever." *Forever* dissolved into a series of shuddering sobs. "And now I've got nobody!"

"Mrs. Lopez," John tried.

"M-m-miss," she managed and then wailed again.

"Miss Lopez—"

"Miss," Emery said—apparently not quietly enough, because John gave him another dirty look.

"Shit, shit, shit," Auggie said as he finally wrenched free of his mother. "I never finished the playlist."

"Jem and I put one together," John said. "Miss Lopez, maybe a drink of water—"

"And I didn't check the spelling on the place cards. God damn it, I told Theo I'd check them."

Emery snorted. "You were going to check them? They're fine; I gave them a final pass before I had them printed. What kind of mail merge software did you use?"

Auggie stared at him, his face frozen and uncomprehending in fresh horror. "Theo's boutonniere."

"What?" John asked.

"I'm going to die alone," Gabby blubbered through a fresh wave of hysterics. One hand groped blindly, trying to recapture Auggie, and he inched out of reach without seeming to realize it. "All my babies are gone, and nobody loves me, and I might as well just die."

"Are you fucking kidding me?" Fer snapped from the doorway. He let himself into the bridal suite and shut the door behind him. In a low, furious voice, he said, "People can hear you. They think somebody's skinning a cat in here."

"I don't care, I don't care. My life is over!"

"Your life is over." Auggie's older brother loomed over her. He looked…well, Emery had to admit he looked good in a black suit and a crisp white shirt. "What are Auggie's friends going to think when a red-eyed, wrinkly faced hag hauls her ass out there and says she's his mom?"

John's eyes got huge.

"Get up," Fer continued. "Fix your makeup. Take a fuckin Xanax or ten. And then get the fuck in your seat and don't make me have to deal with you again. This is Auggie's day, not yours." He waited approximately a heartbeat before he roared, "Move!"

Gabby Lopez flew out of the suite.

Emery made a note to talk to Fer—at an appropriate time, like the reception—about the motivational course based on yelling that he'd been workshopping.

"Why don't we go check on Theo?" John asked. "We'll make sure everything's ok with the boutonniere."

Auggie wiped his eyes and nodded, and Fer gave them a look that was equal parts base-level annoyance and gratitude. Hands on Auggie's shoulders, Fer walked him over to a chair and sat him down as Emery and John left the room.

Guests filled the velvet-cushioned pews in the chapel itself, and the echoes of happy conversation bounced back from the vaulted ceilings. Late morning light through the stained glass washed everything in prismatic colors. John nodded to many of the guests as they made their way across the nave to the pastor's office on the opposite side; a few guests, like Fer and Auggie's mom, had traveled to the wedding, but most of Auggie and Theo's friends were now local. And, Emery noted to himself, many of them were clearly of Auggie's making—exhibit A was the young man with the scruff and heavy brow who was spinning Lana in a circle, with total disregard for the likelihood of sudden and intense vomiting.

In the pastor's office, Theo was pacing a line from the desk to the bookcases on the opposite wall, chewing his thumb nail. He glanced over when they entered and kept pacing. He wore an earthy tweed jacket with a white shirt and a matching floral tie. Jem had done something to his hair and beard—some kind of product, presumably—and the flow of strawberry-blond hair had a quality that Emery could only describe as swooshing. In an irritating way, it reminded him of the men on the clothing websites John sometimes frequented. Often, they had a jacket breezily slung over one shoulder, or they were on a sailboat, or both.

The boutonniere was on the desk, still in its plastic case.

John took out the boutonniere and planted himself in Theo's path. Theo made a face and stopped, his hand falling away from his mouth. As John began the process of fastening the flowers to Theo's lapel, Theo said, "It's too many people." A high, nervous laugh escaped him. "I told Auggie we should have eloped."

"It's a lot of people," John said carefully, his attention still fixed on the boutonniere, "who love you and are here to support you."

"And eat your food and drink your booze," Emery said.

"Ree."

"Do you remember the tab from our wedding? Good God, what possessed you to offer an open bar?"

"There," John said, stepping back and brushing Theo's shoulders. "You look fantastic."

Uncertainty showed in Theo's face.

"You look presentable," Emery said.

For some reason, that seemed to crack Theo open. He laughed, and some of the stiffness went out of his body. "Thank you, Emery." He was silent for a moment. Then he said, "We went to a courthouse in Iowa. In jeans and t-shirts, which now, when I'm saying it, makes me want to hit my head against a wall."

"That was then. This is now."

"Ree's right. That was the right thing for you then. And I think this is the right thing for you now, but if you're having second thoughts…"

Theo shook his head. "No. God, no. It's perfect. It's too perfect. I don't deserve—" His eyes shone, and in a thick voice, he asked, "Am I ruining his life? I just need someone to tell me if I am."

John made a soft noise and took Theo into a hug. Theo's shoulders moved once, and then both men were still for a long time. John said something, and Theo nodded, and then they separated. Emery passed Theo tissues from the pastor's desk, and Theo wiped his eyes and tried to smile.

"God, now everyone's going to think—I don't know. I don't want you to think—" He cut himself off again. "I know how lucky I am."

"It's a big day," John said. "Lots of strong emotions. I was so nervous the day of our wedding, I was about to claw my way out of my skin."

"You would have been calmer if you hadn't tried to make it a surprise."

"Here we go."

"What? It's a fact. I would have helped you with the details, and you would have felt less stressed."

"Yeah, sure. I would have felt less stressed having you help me with the details."

"I hear the tone, John."

Theo gave them a watery grin and dried his eyes again.

"You are a good man," Emery told him. "You are a good partner to him. You're raising a wonderful daughter together. My son thinks you walk on water. And all our lives would be less if you were anyone else, anywhere else. I'm proud you're my friend, Theo. And Auggie is fortunate to have you."

And then, to Emery's horror, Theo started to cry.

John nudged Emery forward, and against his better judgment, he wrapped Theo in a hug.

"Thank you," Theo whispered.

Emery nodded.

When Theo stepped back, he cleaned himself up with a fresh tissue and gave a wobbly laugh. "Ok, a lot of strong emotions. Like, a lot." The music changed, and Theo straightened. "Oh God."

"Ready?" John asked.

Theo nodded.

Emery left John standing at the door to the pastor's office and crossed the nave again. The quartet was playing softly, music Emery didn't recognize, and the hub of voices had quieted. When he reached the bridal suite, he knocked lightly and inched the door open.

"I am so proud of you," Fer was saying, his voice broken. "And I love you more than anyone in the whole world."

Whatever Auggie said back was too quiet for Emery to hear, but then Fer said, "Here we go, Augustus. And try not to look like such a cooz, for Christ's sake."

Fer left first, moving to take his place in the chancel, and a moment later, the music changed again. Emery swung the door open, and Auggie stepped out. Opposite them, John opened the pastor's door, and Theo emerged. Theo and Auggie looked at each other, and for a moment, Emery was fairly certain that nobody else existed in the universe.

They met at the center of the nave, clasped hands, and made their way to the chancel. Fer watched them, his expression unreadable. He produced a piece of paper, glanced down once more at Auggie, and then a smile fractured across his face, and it looked, for a single moment, like he might burst into tears.

"For those of you who don't know me, I'm Fernando, Auggie's brother." He stopped and swallowed, and Emery wondered if anyone listening believed, in that moment, that Fer was only his brother. "On behalf of Theo and Auggie, I want to thank you for being here today to witness and celebrate their love." He stopped again, and that smile cracked across his face again. "What seems like a long time ago, Auggie called me and asked for advice about giving someone a birthday present. I didn't know he was talking about Theo at the time, but I knew something was different, considering the last time Auggie had gotten me a gift, he'd been six, and it had been one of his Transformers that he'd put inside a pillowcase." A laugh rippled through the audience. Auggie started to cry—just a few tears sliding down his cheeks to bracket his smile. "I told Auggie that the best present is one that shows the other person that you know them and care about them. That's my way of saying this wedding must be Theo's gift to me because he's finally taking Auggie off my hands." Another laugh rolled through the congregation. Fer's smile trembled like it was about to slide off. Auggie was crying harder, but his smile shone through the tears.

As Fer launched into the usual platitudes about love and marriage, fidelity and responsibility, Emery relaxed against the wall. He ought to have been surprised when John appeared at his side and laced their fingers together, but he wasn't.

"Now we're at the most important part," Fer said. "Do you, August Paul Lopez, take Daniel Theophilus Stratford to be your lawfully wedded spouse, to honor and to cherish him from this day forward, sharing your life through good times and bad, offering kindness, patience, and comfort each day, for as long as love shall last?"

Auggie wiped his eyes and said, "I do."

"And do you, Daniel Theophilus Stratford, take August Paul Lopez to be your lawfully wedded spouse, to honor and to cherish him from this day forward, sharing your life through good times and bad, offering kindness, patience, and comfort each day, for as long as love shall last?"

Nodding, Theo said in a choked voice, "Yes."

"How about an 'I do'?" Fer prompted.

Chuckles broke up the moment. Theo seemed to relax, and he smiled as he looked at Auggie and said, "I do."

"I believe we have some rings," Fer said.

Evie and Lana hustled from their seats in the front row. Evie passed her ring to Auggie and spun around so quickly that she almost fell as she darted back to her chair. But Lana took her time, leaning into Theo to hug him after she gave him the ring, and then repeating the gesture with Auggie before returning to her seat.

"And we'd better have some vows," Fer said.

Auggie spoke first. "Theo, getting to know you, falling in love with you, and having the chance to spend my life with you has been the single greatest blessing of my life. You're patient with me. You're kind. You work so hard for our family. And it probably shouldn't surprise anyone that when we met, you were my teacher, because you've taught me so much. One thing I've learned from you—maybe the most important thing—is to cherish every moment, because you never know what the future holds. So, there are a lot of things I want to promise you. I want to promise that I'll sweep up the Doritos crumbs like we've talked about. And I want to promise that I'll be better about the peanut butter knife—I really will. I'll be the best dad to Lana that I can be, and as much as you'll let me, I'll take care of you too. But the most important promise I make to you today is that I'm here with you, for as long as we have each other, and whatever comes, we'll get through it together. I love you, and I will never take anything for granted—not you, not your love, and not this life we're building together." Auggie's hands were shaking as he reached for Theo's and slid the ring into place.

Theo tightened his hands around Auggie's before he spoke. "Shakespeare ended his comedies with weddings—"

From the back of the chapel came a loud, "Boo!"

North.

But everyone burst out laughing, even Theo, and Auggie laughed so hard that he almost fell and had to lean into Theo. When the room quieted, Theo said, "Shakespeare ended his comedies with weddings, but they usually began in disaster. When I met you, Auggie, my life was a disaster. And now here I am, and I think I'm living a comedy. Not the ha-ha kind, but the stories that remind people that kindness and grace and love can be salvaged from the darkest nights, that devastation is not destiny, that life, as they say, can go on." He stopped, struggling with a wave of emotion, and when he spoke again, his voice was rough. "So, in that spirit, I want to promise you that I will never give up on you, or on me, or on us. And every day, I will try to show you how grateful I am for you, and for my life with you, and for how you brought a light into my darkness when I thought there was nothing left for me. I promise that I will do everything I can to be a good husband, to take care of you, and to make sure you know how much I love you. Because even though this is a wedding, this isn't the end of our story.

It's just the next part." His hands tightened around Auggie's for a heartbeat, and then he released him and slid the ring into place.

Fer wiped his eyes, and in a thick voice, he said, "Now how the fuck am I supposed to say anything after that?" But as the chorus of laughs faded, he said, "Theo and Auggie, by virtue of the authority vested in me by the state of Missouri, I now pronounce you married." A smirk canted across his lips. "Go ahead and kiss, dummies. This is officially your happily ever after."

Acknowledgments

My deepest thanks go out to the following people (in alphabetical order):

Marie Lenglet, for her help with clarity, so many typos, and the timeline of the final vigrettes.

Mark Wallace, for catching my missing words, for asking about those ambiguous pronouns, and for lending his reader brain with those wonderful thoughts about the family interactions in these stories.

And special thanks to Alicia, Alyssa, Christine, Raye, and Ruth for catching additional errors in the ARC!

About the Author

For advanced access, exclusive content, limited-time promotions, and insider information, please sign up for my mailing list at **www.gregoryashe.com**.